Anderson Public Library
Lawrenceburg, KY 40342

TAMMY HILL

D1506988

KNOWING

a series of gifts

CREATION
HOUSE

Knowing: A Series of Gifts by Tammy Hill
Published by Creation House
A Charisma Media Company
600 Rinehart Road
Lake Mary, Florida 32746
www.charismamedia.com

This book or parts thereof may not be reproduced in any form, stored in a retrieval system, or transmitted in any form by any means—electronic, mechanical, photocopy, recording, or otherwise—without prior written permission of the publisher, except as provided by United States of America copyright law.

All Scripture quotations are from the Holy Bible, New Living Translation, copyright © 1996, 2004, 2007 by Tyndale House Foundation. Used by permission of Tyndale House Publishers Inc., Carol Stream, Illinois, 60188. All rights reserved.

Names appearing in this text have been changed to preserve the anonymity of the individuals. Any similarity to actual persons is coincidental and unintended by the publisher.

Design Director: Bill Johnson
Cover concept and photography by Tammy Hill
Cover design by Nancy Panaccione

Copyright © 2012 by Tammy Hill
All rights reserved

Visit the author's website: www.aseriesofgifts.com

Library of Congress Cataloging-in-Publication Data: 2012931522
International Standard Book Number: 978-1-61638-926-0
E-book International Standard Book Number: 978-1-61638-927-7

While the author has made every effort to provide accurate telephone numbers and Internet addresses at the time of publication, neither the publisher nor the author assumes any responsibility for errors or for changes that occur after publication.

12 13 14 15 16 — 9 8 7 6 5 4 3
Printed in the United States of America

D e d i c a t i o n

....

To my children:
Your strength and your courage to overcome inspire me.

Table of Contents

....

A spiritual gift is given to each of us so we can help each other.

—1 CORINTHIANS 12:7

 *Prologue*

MY DREAM HAUNTS me, and not only when I am asleep. It also scratches the back of my wakened mind, as elusive as a forgotten lyric or name and yet, it leaves me in a state of perpetual hunger; searching for something I know is close but just out of my reach.

This recurring nightmare never deviates for a moment. As always, I lay on my stomach across my bed in my old bedroom, engrossed in the book that lies open in front of me. Sheltered in the pastel pink of my room, I am always oblivious in the beginning. My bare feet move lazily from the bed and back heavenward as I bend my legs with each turn of the page, humming a tuneless melody. Although there is nothing alarming; no sound or movement other than my own; a sense of unease washes over me. My heart begins to thud loudly in my chest and my veins turn to ice as I slowly move to a sitting position in my bed.

Then, my walls crumble to the floor in one swift movement as silently as a curtain dropping after the final act. I jump up and stare in disbelief at what I see around me. No longer protected by the false security of my walls, I see a wasteland of charred earth and darkness. A whimper escapes me and tears spring to my eyes. I turn in a circle looking for a place to hide, but everything from my past life is gone now; only destruction and ruin remain. Just beyond the darkness, I can barely make out the shadows of horrific creatures. I can't help but to close my eyes to them. Then, the screams begin. I hear hundreds of voices, all screaming in pain and pleading for help. As I cower in the place that was once my safe haven, I have a strong feeling of urgency to do something. Even in my fear, I know the answer is close. I fall to the ground, kneeling over with my arms bent over my head. I rock back and forth like this, pleading to someone for the answer all the while knowing I should get up and help these lost souls.

I know.

Then, as quickly as the revelation began, it's over. I wake up with my heart pounding, gasping for air, knowing inherently things aren't what they seem. I wake up knowing that I have a purpose to fulfill. Soon though, the dream fades, along with the feeling of urgency. Although the desire for answers never leaves me, my everyday life begins to take precedence over the fervor of my dream.

Once again, I'm lulled into believing that I'm just an average, powerless teenager.

Chapter One

I RECLINED ON THE beach towel and grabbed another to throw over my face. I had only just taken a few steps out of the ocean, but the drops of water were already baking off my sun-darkened skin. I blindly groped for the small, red cooler positioned between my cousin and me. I should have gotten out a bottle of water before I covered my face; dilemmas like this were the extent of my problems nowadays. I found the bottle and pulled it out, ignoring the mumbling of my fifteen-year-old cousin, whom I had evidently splashed with ice water. As the older by a year, I had been looking out for her this summer; she could consider this my aiding her against heatstroke.

I leaned up on my elbows to take a sip. The towel fell from my face, so I glanced around at the carefree families playing in the surf and then took a minute to check out the guys as they checked out the girls. I had been staying with my grandparents at their house on the beach for four weeks now; it had become a familiar scene. I tunneled my toes further down to find the damp coolness in the white sand as the DJ on our small portable stereo talked about the record-breaking heat. In the distance, I could hear a gang of squawking seagulls demanding more food from the unfortunate tourist who made the mistake of tossing up the first crumb. Further off, there was the occasional crack of a firecracker, leftovers from last weekend's Fourth of July celebration.

I looked over for my bag so I could toss the now empty bottle, but didn't see it. Instead, I caught a glance of my grandfather waving to me from the boardwalk. It was not just a friendly wave. Instead, it yelled, *I need you for something*! My cell phone was securely zipped up in plastic and tucked away in our beach bag, wherever that was. I nudged Priscilla, who must have been in a sun coma, because she didn't budge. I reached in the cooler and doused her again, which snapped her right out of it. She didn't think it was funny, to say the least, and was a little too smug for my liking when she told me the bag, along with my cell phone, was in the house. Now it was my turn to grumble as I threw my swimsuit cover over my head. Then, I realized my flip-flops were also in the absent bag. I would have to attempt to jog up to the beach house without burning my feet on the white-hot sand. I skeptically judged the distance. I told you I had problems.

"Hi, Gramps, what's up?" I asked from the wooden steps just outside the screened back porch where he stood. I reached over and twisted on the short water faucet. It let out a squeak in reply. I used the attached green hose to spray off my legs and feet; a ritual my grandmother expected us to perform each time we made the short walk from the beach.

"Ember, I hate to tell you this, but it looks like we're going to have to cut your stay with us a little short."

I hope it will only be by a few days, I thought, as I opened the screen door. I had been having a great time. When I asked him how short was short, he ran a hand through his thinning hair.

"Well, I just talked to your mom. She wants you back tomorrow."

There was about a five second moment of shocked silence, then I exploded, "Tomorrow, but that's ridiculous!" I began shuffling around sofa pillows, looking for the lost cell phone bag with urgency, already concocting arguments with Mom in my mind. I found the missing beach bag lying on the floor behind a chair. I pulled out the baggie and held it up, grinning from my victory; until I noticed Granddad didn't share my excitement. He had taken a seat on the porch swing and was just looking down at his tented fingers.

"Granddad," I asked with a sense of unease. "Is everything OK?" He just smiled and patted the empty spot beside him.

"Honey, everything is fine. Everyone is healthy." I let out a deep breath in relief because he had answered the question I was afraid to ask. My grandfather smiled again to reassure me.

As I remember it now, I realize his eyes didn't match his smile's optimism, but I was—to make a grand understatement—a lot less "in tune" back then.

"I didn't want to be the one to tell you this...," he hesitated, looking over at the back door. My gaze followed his to my grandmother, who was watching us through the window. Realizing she had been discovered, she quickly wiped her hands on her apron and came out, taking a seat in the rocking chair. "...but, your mom wanted you to know now and not over the telephone."

Grandma broke in. "Just say it, George, you're scaring her."

"Grace, if you think you could do better..."

"Please, you two, what's wrong?" I pleaded.

Grandma shot him a scathing look and filled me in on what would be yet another life changing transition for me. "Your mother has divorced Bill, honey. It looks like they decided to end it the last time you were here, during spring break. The papers were finalized last week." She paused and glanced nervously at me then continued, more brightly, "It sounds like Kim's found a cute little place for you two, just a few miles outside of the city. She needs our help to get some of your things moved in and, of course, we're happy to help. I've already talked to your uncles. They're willing to take off the next couple of days and go with us. They'll just have to work the weekend to make it up, but their boss is always real understanding about family matters…"

She was just rambling now, graciously giving me time to wrap my head around the unexpected news. My mother had left my stepfather. Four years ago, almost to the day, they were getting married on this beach; now it was over. Grandma used the words, "cute and little" when she described the house. Knowing Mom, she had refused to take much financial help from Bill, if any at all, even though he was loaded. I took a deep, shaky breath. So, the life of popularity and wealth was over, just like that. I tasted the salty tears before I sensed I was crying. Grandma must have realized it at the same time because she stopped chattering. She and Grandpa both jumped up and sandwiched me into a fierce hug.

"I'm so sorry, sweetheart. I can't believe they did this to you. It's going to be all right. We'll help you through this…"

On and on it went, these words of encouragement she and Granddad cooed at me through my tears. What they didn't know—couldn't understand—was their pity fell on deaf ears.

I was crying tears of relief.

The movement of the swing lulled me into numbness as I sat on the screened back porch of my new house. The rain mimicked my mood and took the place of the tears I no longer had in me to shed. Only yesterday, I was enjoying the summer at my grandparents' beach house in Florida. We had planned for me to stay until mid-August, but it was cut a month short by Mom's insistence to get out of my stepfather's house. I mean *ex*-stepfather. Instead of an address in the wealthy area of Atlanta, we now resided on the outskirts in Smalltown, USA, population 15,000. I know he was helping her financially because she was able to get a day job in a pediatric clinic instead of the many shifts she used to work before Dr. Bill. He wasn't exactly throwing money at her feet, though, considering we were the proud owners of a 1950s brick ranch house, roughly only a little larger than a mobile home.

After the long drive, my grandparents, uncles, and I stayed in a rundown hotel by the interstate. My grandmother and I slept in the same room, though only one of us actually got any sleep. I spent the night with a pillow over my head in a futile attempt to drown out the sounds of my grandmother's snores and the neighbor's television that blared all night through the paper-thin walls. We had an early morning rendezvous in the lobby for breakfast. Soon, we were on the road to my new house and life. I wasn't ready, but cold cereal from a plastic dispenser in a room the size of closet didn't exactly inspire anyone to hang out. Besides, they were all here to work. After a surprisingly quick reunion with Mom and an even faster tour of the house, everyone went to work unloading the moving van. Thankfully, the carport kept us from getting too soaked and we managed to unload all of the boxes and put the furniture in place. My family left to get an early dinner and to help Mom return the rental truck before heading back to Florida. I said my goodbyes and stayed at the house to sulk. I just wanted to be alone for a while and process everything. I had spent my time staring at nothing, lost in the past. When I came out of it I noticed, for

the first time, a dead plant in the corner of the porch. The previous owners must have left it behind. I couldn't blame them. It
obviously hadn't seen water for days; no way it was coming back
to life. In spite of my better judgment, I picked it up and put it
outside in the rain. We all deserve another chance.

Just as I got comfortable again, the sliding glass door opened.
I turned to see Mom standing there, shaking her head.

"Daydreaming again, Ember? What's the fantasy about this
time?" she joked.

"That I have my life back," I retorted and felt instantly sorry,
but pride kept me quiet.

Mom's face fell. She looked as if she wanted to say more, but
we were interrupted by a guy who looked about my age carrying
one of our boxes of stuff.

"Where would you like this?"

Mom asked him to set it on the table for a minute. "Ember,
this is Cade. He rode by, saw me unloading this box we missed,
and insisted on helping."

Cade walked over to me and stuck out his hand. "Hi, I'm
Cade," then rolled his eyes at his mistake.

"Yeah, I heard. And as you heard, I'm Ember," I said, still
grumpy from being disturbed. I saw the appalled look on Mom's
face and took the hint. I reached out and gave his hand a quick
squeeze.

"With an E?" he asked, seemingly unfazed by my rudeness.

"Yeah, my parents had a weird sense of humor."

He laughed at my misfortune and then grinned, not taking
his eyes off of me. I surprised myself by smiling back. I couldn't
seem to help myself. The guy practically radiated crush vibes.
Plus, he was cute with sun-lightened, thick blond hair cut in
uneven layers, blue eyes, and a 100-watt, mischievous smile.

Mom cleared her throat, and I dragged my eyes away to check the box.

"That goes to my room. Come on, I'll show you."

My "new" room had obviously been decorated for a little boy. It was powder blue from the ceiling down to the shag carpet and was about the size of a box. In fact, the entire house could almost fit into my closet. The closet that used to be mine, that is; in the life I lived for four years beginning when I was twelve. In here, there was a double closet with a sliding door just to the left of the doorway. Straight ahead was a large picture window that took up most of the wall. Underneath it was my twin bed. A full-sized bed wouldn't have fit in here. On the right, by the door, was my mirrored dresser. Further over on the far wall was my memory collector, a white shelving system that took up a full wall. It was comprised of dozens of different-sized cubbies. My grandfather had assembled it for me that morning. I had hoped to put off organizing my things until another day but it looked like fate had a different idea.

"Keep the door open!" Mom instructed loudly from the kitchen.

I rolled my eyes at the reprimand. "That is so not like her," I informed Cade. Maybe it was the extra stress. I let it go and stepped out of his way. "Just lay it over by the shelves."

"Wow, what are you going to put in here?" he asked, as he placed the box on the floor and took his place by it.

I knelt in front of the box and, once again, found myself smiling, "You have no idea."

When I leaned over the box to open it, a few curls escaped from behind my ear, which is usual for me. It's thick, wavy, and falls a few inches below my shoulders. My hair was normally brown, but the summer sun (and an Atlanta hair colorist) made it lighter with blond highlights. Sunlight, both real and artificial, also darkened my usual porcelain-colored skin, which my mom said made my green eyes "pop," whatever that means. I pulled a hair tie from my wrist and tied my hair back in a knot. I looked up to find Cade staring at me. He quickly looked away. I continued working on the box. I tore it open and brushed away Styrofoam popcorn to reveal my treasure.

"What is all of this?" Cade asked reaching inside.

"Memories," I responded with pride and pulled out a Statue of Liberty snow globe. "My bio-dad brought me this after one of his trips."

"Bio-dad?"

"Yeah, my biological father, Jackson Matthews. He and my mother dated in high school. He was tall, dark, and handsome and wanted to see the world right after graduation. She was underage and smitten, but knew her parents would never approve, so they eloped. That summer, they made it from Florida to Atlanta before they found out Mom was pregnant with me. He left the summer after I was born to 'explore their next options' and finally only came back to give her divorce papers."

"That bites. So, you don't see him often?"

I shook my head and placed the globe on a shelf. "He has four different kids from four different wives. That and his wanderlust keep him busy, and absent. That's why the few things I do have from him are special. He's never been there to give me any other kind of memories."

"And this?" Cade asked as he held a little, white Bible.

I took it and thumbed through it, smiling. "I received that as a gift from my old church when I got water baptized. That was right before Mom got remarried to Bill. I was twelve. I don't think I've ever felt happier than I did that night," I whispered, lost in the memory.

"So, you're a Christian?"

"Yes. I mean a lot has happened since then, but that doesn't matter, right?" I asked, chewing my lip.

Cade shrugged. "Don't ask me. I don't get into that stuff." I guess he noticed my concern at his abrupt behavior because he added, "Look, I totally understand your need for religion, especially when you were young and weak. I just don't need that right now in my life. Everything is going great for me."

"How so?" I prodded.

"I'm going to be a junior this year. That means only two more years of this place, then I'm outta here."

"I'm going to be in eleventh grade, too," I offered. Our eyes locked for a second then he reached around his neck and unclasped his necklace. It was a black leather strip with some kind of gem as the pendant. He slid the pendant off, stood up and laid it on the top shelf.

"What are you doing?"

"This is definitely a good memory kind of day," he said with a wink. I'd better get going. If you want to talk church with someone you should meet Mouse."

"Mouse?" I questioned.

"Yeah, I think you two will really hit it off. You want me to introduce you to her and show you around some tomorrow?"

"I would like that," I said happily, as I stood up.

Cade asked for my cell number and dialed it to send me his number. On the way out, he paused at my doorway and said, "I know this must be rough on you, moving and all, so you'll just have to forgive me."

"For what?" I asked, puzzled.

"For taking pleasure in your pain. I'll call you later tonight, new girl" he said with a smile and left me alone with the butterflies in my stomach. I blinked as a glare bounced off my mirror. I turned around to face the window.

"So there you are," I said to the setting sun with a grin.

C h a p t e r   T w o

T HE NEXT MORNING, I poured myself a bowl of cereal and made my way into the living room. I plopped down sideways in the armchair and studied the sad condition of the room. It had dark paneling on the walls and gold shag carpet on the floors. A half-wall divided the living area from the entryway. The top portion of the so-called wall had spindles to the ceiling, giving the impression of a jail cell. Mom came in as I was scrutinizing the décor and recognized the look on my face.

"It will get better, you know," she said as she sat on the couch and looked around as if she could already see the difference. "We just moved in yesterday, but I already have a lot of plans for this place. The room feels dark and small, but the huge windows will bring in a lot of light with a good wash and once we paint it a lighter color...you'll see," she added, cutting her plans of grandeur off short.

I looked over and saw unshed tears fill her eyes. "Oh Mom," I said. She opened her arms to me, so I put down my bowl and curled up in her arms beside her.

"I'm so sorry, baby. I know this has to be so hard for you. It's such a change from what you've been used to for the past few years."

"I just don't understand. Why so sudden?" I asked. "I'm assuming everything went downhill during spring break when you sent me to Grandma's." Her nod confirmed my belief. "Did Bill do something terrible?" I asked. He and I were never close, primarily because he was always working, but I'd always thought he was a nice guy.

"No, no . . . nothing like that," she answered wiping away tears. "It wasn't him; it was me. Don't look at me like that, Jacqueline Ember. I know it sounds cliché, but it's true." Sighing, she took her arm away and leaned back on the other side of the couch, facing me. "You're sixteen now, so I don't want to oversimplify things, but it is simple. I just didn't fit there. It wasn't me. Bill came from a long line of wealthy relatives while I was raised in a modest, middle class home. I barely made it out of high school and was a pregnant teenager." Mom hugged her knees and continued sadly. "As the saying goes, 'You can put lipstick on a pig . . .'"

"Mom, don't even finish that," I insisted. "Bill fell in love with you because you are an intelligent, strong person. You raised a daughter on your own while working two jobs and going through nursing school. Not to mention the fact that you're also a beautiful woman." She rolled her eyes at my observation, but it was true. Mom looks fragile with her fair skin, short blond hair, blue eyes, and small frame, but she has more tenacity than a bulldog.

"Whatever the reasons are that we fell in love with each other, I knew I had made a mistake within weeks of our marriage. I did try to stay, especially when I saw how you were thriving; private school, all those music, art, and dance lessons, and time to spend with friends without having to worry about money. I knew I could never give you that on my own. For four years I lived trying to be the perfect doctor's wife, we even tried counseling. But you're right, by spring I just..." She struggled for the words, but I already understood what she was saying.

"It's OK, Mom. I understand. Bill is a nice guy, but I know he put pressure on you to be someone you're not," I said, reaching over to pat her hand.

"I came in here on a mission to make you feel better," she said as she reached across me to grab a tissue from the side table. "I should have known it would work the other way around. You have always understood people, Ember. You have a gift."

I blew off her last comment and decided to go for complete honesty. "I know I've been sulky today so you probably won't believe me, but I'm actually kind of happy for it to be just you and me again, Mom," I confessed.

"Then why do you seem so down?" she asked.

"I just feel like there is something more...something I'm supposed to be doing with my life."

"Oh, no," she interrupted. "You are not old enough to be going through a midlife crisis, young lady!" she insisted and kissed my forehead. "Whatever is going on with you, maybe a blond-haired guy might help you through it," she said with a wink. "You two stayed on the phone long enough last night to figure out how to accomplish world peace."

We *had* talked until late last night, but it was more on a personal level. I blushed and said, "No. It's not like that. Mom, there's something else. I've been having this same dream; a nightmare," I began, but was interrupted by the chirp of my cell phone.

Mom looked over my shoulder, said, "Speak of the devil...," and with a smug look, stood up to leave. "We'll talk more later," she promised.

After realizing she could hear us last night, I waited until she was clanging around in the kitchen to answer the phone. Cade was calling to see if I was ready to "hit the town." I looked down at my boxer shorts, tank top, and fluffy slippers with rising panic. "You're not on your way now…are you?" I squeaked.

He was ready, but thankfully still at home, and would wait for my call to come over. We said a quick good-bye, then I ran into the kitchen, my slippers clacking loudly on the faux wooden floor, to throw my cereal bowl in the sink. I ignored Mom's smile as I made a mad dash for the shower.

I called Cade while I was drying off. By the time I emerged from my room, he was sitting at the kitchen table with my mom, having a glass of orange juice and chatting. He had on khaki shorts loaded with pockets and a tight fitting black t-shirt with a video game decal in the center. When Cade noticed me standing there, a look of genuine admiration flashed across his face, which thrilled me. I guess some people have made positive comments about my looks. I think I'm just average though, average height, 5'6", and a normal build. I'm certainly not skinny. Mom says I have a little baby fat left. I play nice and go along with her delusion, though we both know it should have been gone long ago. Regardless of what anyone else thought about me, the way Cade looked at me made me feel like model material, even in shorts and a t-shirt. It was the only ensemble fitting for the intense summer heat that I could already feel radiating through the glass door.

We said bye to Mom and left through the laundry room, which connects to the kitchen and exits to the carport. We both looked at each other expectantly. "I guess we didn't discuss travel arrangements," I quipped.

"Do you drive?"

"No. I have my learner's permit, but Mom refused to take me back after my first failed attempt and Bill never had time. They were supposed to give me a car for my sixteenth birthday, of course. I ended up spending it in Florida, so it just didn't work out." I plopped down in a camping chair and fiddled with one of the seams.

"It didn't seem that big of a deal at the time. All my friends had cars so there was no shortage of rides, you know? I guess it's a big deal now, though.

"Nah. Don't sweat it. Do you have a bike?"

I nodded, grabbed Mom's bike and walked it out to the driveway where he was standing by his ten-speed. "You don't drive, either?" I asked as I put on my helmet.

"Definitely," he replied, throwing his leg over the bike. "I totaled my Jeep last week when some of us guys were out racing in the woods. My parents are shopping for a new truck for me as we speak," he bragged.

"And you didn't want to help pick it out?" I questioned in disbelief.

"Of course I did," he admitted, "but it's Saturday, the only day they have off to shop."

When I looked at him perplexed, he continued, "There was no way I was going to miss being with you." With that, he rode away and left me staring dumbly after him with a silly smile on my face. "You coming, new girl?" he yelled back over his shoulder.

"Absolutely" I said to no one and took off after him.

I caught up with Cade and we kept a leisurely pace through the pine-filled neighborhood of small houses that all looked similar to mine. After a few turns and a couple of rolling hills, the homes became newer and there were more with two stories.

Cade signaled a left turn and whizzed into the driveway of a white, wooden house with dark green shutters. A large magnolia tree shaded most of the well-manicured front yard. A pretty flowerbed accompanied stepping-stones to a small covered front entrance. I followed Cade's lead as he parked in front of the garage and got off the bike. I took off my helmet and tried to straighten my hair.

"Is this where Mouse lives? I feel stupid calling her that, by the way. What is her real name?" I questioned.

"No, and I don't remember anymore," he said with a shrug.

"You're kidding me," I responded to both answers. "I thought you wanted to introduce us; 'you will really hit it off,'" I mocked, giving my best Cade impression.

He stepped up on the porch and turned back to face me. "I also said I wanted to spend the day with you. Forgive me for not being ready to share you just yet," he joked and turned to the door.

I followed behind him with a bounce in my step to find him trying different keys in the lock. "Wait, hold on. So this is your house?" I asked. "And your parents are gone?"

He opened the door and held it for me. "Yes and yes. I won't do a thing to you, I promise. I just want to show you around."

I knew Mom wouldn't be happy about my going in, but quite honestly, I had done a lot worse in the last four years. I wanted a fresh start, which was the cause of my hesitation, but felt silly when he looked at me in confusion.

"What? Are you afraid of me?" he asked in disbelief.

"No, of course not," I responded and followed him inside.

Blinking as my eyes adjusted, I was welcomed by a poster home for middle-class, two-parent Americans. I liked it. In fact, my earlier concerns were unfounded. Cade gave me a quick tour of the four-bedroom home, which included a huge, lazy Persian cat that refused to move from the couch and a very excited black Lab that ran laps around the inground pool to prove her excitement to see us.

"Hi, Raven. You're a good girl, aren't you?" cooed Cade as he petted his dog. He threw a stick near the pool and Raven took off after it. I must have looked at the sparkling water with longing because Cade asked if I wanted to take a swim. The Georgia heat was intensifying, but I reluctantly told him no.

"Water would be great, though," I said, trying to hide my disappointment over my own decision.

Cade and I sat on the floor in the living room and leaned against his floral printed sofa. We sipped our water bottles and took turns petting—here's a stretch—Snowball. I discovered Cade had an older sister who was away at university. He insisted that his parents were just waiting for him to leave the nest so they could retire from their state government jobs and see the States from the front seat of a Winnebago. I thought he was being a bit dramatic, but he swore it was true. At least I understood his desire to leave a little better. If the parents were selling out, it would make sense for him to look for another place to crash. I also learned about his childhood, which was the All-American variety: Boy Scouts, baseball, and quite a few crushes. He hedged toward asking me about guys whom I've dated. In truth, I *had* dated a lot of guys, but they didn't mean anything to me. The reality seemed too coldhearted to admit, so I just shook my head and hoped Cade would let it drop. He didn't.

"You were with someone though, right? There is no way guys didn't go for you," Cade determined.

I laughed at his conviction. "Yeah, there were guys who liked me. I guess you could call them boyfriends. It's not like you think, though." He raised his eyebrows, waiting for me to clarify. "I dated guys who the plastics thought I should."

"Plastics?" he inquired.

"It's just a name I called the popular girls; the ones who took me in and showed me the ropes when I went from 'poor girl' to 'poor, rich girl.'"

"Wow, you sounded scary when you said that. Talk about anger issues," Cade joked.

"Actually, to say they showed me the ropes was being nice. The plastics just wanted to make me a copy of them," I responded. No longer able to look him in the eye, I resumed petting Snowball. "I really don't want to talk about this right now," I commanded but my shaky voice gave me away.

I felt Cade's cool hand against my cheek and looked at him, embarrassed to feel a tear slide onto his fingers. I froze like that for an instant, looking into his eyes while feeling my heart pounding in my chest. He leaned forward slightly and stopped. He got up and held out his hand to me.

"I promised," he said in a whisper tainted with regret.

It took me a moment to remember what he said at the front door. I took his hand and we walked out. He locked the door, never letting go of my hand until it was time to get back on the bikes.

My aching muscles eased my mind of the embarrassment of baring my soul to Cade, while the unbearable heat kept the memory of his air-conditioned home and pool near and dear to my heart. I was about to yell for a break when we turned left onto Main Street. I had arrived in town on Thursday evening, so I had missed seeing downtown. My imagination didn't do justice to what I considered a small Southern town, while this street was the epitome of it. Tall, flat-faced brick buildings with brightly colored awnings stretched along each side of the two-way street. Black street lamps accented its sidewalks, still displaying American flags from Independence Day; or maybe the flags were permanent fixtures representing this town's pride year round. The sidewalks were full of lunchtime pedestrians leisurely strolling by, glancing occasionally in the large windows that held the sellers' wares, but primarily their attention was on their fellow idlers. They greeted the other with a tip of their head or a smile. I noticed a few whispered covertly when the other was out of earshot.

I didn't realize I had pulled over and was staring at the scene before me until I noticed Cade madly waving his hands up the street. I walked my bike up to him and we rested both of them on a wall. According to the large white letters on the huge window, we were at "Johnson's Family Cooking Cafeteria." Cade had already opened the door for me and was letting out cool air, so I quickly ducked inside. Once again, I was struck by the Southern charm of this place. There were numerous ceiling fans trying desperately to win against the July heat. On the left side of the restaurant were rows of booths. Friendly faces smiled up at us and greeted Cade as we walked toward the back. The rest of the sitting area was filled with tables; each had a unique floral tablecloth with a flower in a small vase and a pitcher of iced tea. I could hear a song coming through the speakers. Some singer lamented about the pain of a lost love while a steel guitar whined along in agreement.

Cade led me to the back, stopping often to return greetings and introduce me. We finally made it to the back wall where the cafeteria line was located. We each took a tray and waited our turn to move our trays down the metal track.

"Meat and three," he said. "My treat."

I was going to argue about the bill, but a woman behind the counter was already asking for my first selection. By the time I had moved to the end of our destination, the cash register, my tray was loaded down with fried chicken, mashed potatoes and gravy, fried okra, squash casserole, and fried cornbread. I looked down incredulous at the amount of food no human could ever be expected to finish. Cade must have noticed my incredulous look because he glanced at my overflowing plate and said smiling, "Don't worry; I'll eat what you can't." I highly doubted it considering the mountain of meatloaf I saw stacked on his plate, but just shrugged, waited for him to pay, and followed him to a booth.

I made it through a third of the food and watched, with a mixture of disbelief and awe, Cade dive into my leftovers with gusto. As he pigged out, a petite, cute girl our age slid into the booth next to Cade. She ran her hands through her unruly brown hair and smiled shyly at me from the top of her black-framed glasses. She gave him a quick jab in the side with her elbow, which made him turn his attention away from the food.

"Ow!" he exclaimed. When the girl only looked at him expectantly, Cade put down his fork, wiped his mouth on the napkin from his lap, and introduced us.

"Ember, this is Mouse; Mouse, Ember," he added, gesturing to me across the table. His job done, Cade turned his attention back to his commandeered plate of food, leaving me awkwardly facing his silent, smiling friend. I noticed she was wearing a white apron so I took the leap and asked her if she worked there.

"Yes" was all she offered.

I looked to Cade for help.

He sighed and continued for her, "Mouse's family owns the place. She's been working here for as long as I can remember."

Then to his friend, he scolded, "Ember is nice, Mouse. You don't have to be so quiet around her."

"I'd better get to work," was all she said in response to his lecture. I thought that was the end of it, but once she got out of the booth she quietly added, "It was nice to meet you, Ember. I get off work in an hour," and quickly made her way through the guests to the kitchen.

I noticed no one tried to speak to her. Cade saw me watching her walk away and said, "She is really only shy around people she doesn't know."

Once again I doubted him, but, eyeing the two empty plates, I realized he had proved me wrong once today. *Actually, twice,* I thought. I remembered his promise at his house and felt my cheeks heat up in response.

I ignored his questioning look and replied, "Oh well, I guess I got my answer to why you call her Mouse."

He laughed as we slid out of the booth. Cade grabbed my hand and we made our way out of the restaurant and into the sweltering heat of the early afternoon.

"So where to now, O great tour guide?" I joked as we got back on our bikes.

"We only have an hour and it has to be somewhere cool. You wanna get an ice cream?" he asked.

"You've got to be kidding!" I countered, holding my stomach in mock pain.

"Fine. There is only one other way to beat this heat. Come back in for a second and wait for me," he said, holding open the door to the restaurant again.

I leaned against the gumball machines just inside the door and waited for Cade as he walked toward the line. He hung up his phone just as he reached me. "We're all set. Let's go," he said cheerfully.

"Go where?" I asked.

"Back to your house," he said and then paused as he straddled the bike, "for your swimsuit." With a wink, he waited for me then we pedaled our way toward home.

We found Mom leaning over several paint swatches that were scattered all over the kitchen table.

"Hi, Mrs. Watson," Cade said. I wondered how he knew how to address her, but then remembered the two of them had met before.

Mom looked up with a smile then exclaimed, "Oh my goodness! The two of you look like you're on the verge of heatstroke! Have you been out walking in this heat?"

"Riding our bikes, actually, but I hope that was the last time I ever have to take only two wheels for transportation." I guess he knew my next question because he continued, "Mom and Dad are home. They said my truck will be at the lot tomorrow."

"That's great news, Cade," I said, genuinely happy for him (and more than a little relieved to have a solution to getting around in the heat). He looked like he wanted to say more, but the water bottles Mom pressed into our hands kind of ruined the moment.

Neither of you is going anywhere until you cool down," she announced.

"But Mom, I'm fine. I would really like to meet his parents. Plus, he has a pool." I am ashamed to say that I whined a bit, but I was feeling a little nauseous.

"Both of you go to the couch right now. I'm going to bring you some cool, damp towels for your heads. Once you're out of danger, I'll drive you two over to Cade's."

"Thanks," we both mumbled and dragged ourselves to the living room to spread out on the couch.

After a few minutes of cool air and some Tylenol, we were as good as new. In reality, it took me longer to decide between a one or two-piece swimsuit than it took to recover from "heatstroke." I remembered the lunch I had consumed only an hour earlier and made the wise decision—the whole piece. It was the same color green as my eyes, was cut high enough on my thighs to make my legs look longer, and had a racer back so I didn't have to worry about a "wardrobe malfunction"—not that I had to be too concerned anyway. Like with everything else with me, I was average in the cleavage department, too. One glance in the mirror and I made the wise decision to take a shower. I took a quick one and looked through unpacked boxes to find something else to wear since the clothes I had on were gross. I didn't have to worry about riding a bike, so I chose a cute, light, floral sundress that went just below my knees. I put my hair into a ponytail, threw my swimsuit in my backpack and went out to let them know I was ready.

Mom led us out to her Mercedes. I noticed Cade didn't try to hold my hand, which I was thankful for. It felt nice to be with him, but I knew Mom would have questions that I wasn't sure I knew the answers to yet. The simple act of walking out on the carport made my head throb again. I sat in the back so Cade could help with directions to his house.

He looked back at me and smiled. "Mouse is going to be there too, you know."

"Really?" I asked. I wasn't sure how I felt about that. She seemed sweet, but I didn't really like uncomfortable silences. Maybe the awkwardness I felt with Mouse was more apparent because of the complete opposite experience I had with Cade. I felt so comfortable with him. I enjoyed the time in the backseat because I could look at him unabashedly. I thought so, anyway.

I looked over to see Mom's eyes looking back at me in the rear-view mirror. Her eyes weren't smiling this time, though. I saw concern in them.

Cade pointed out his house to Mom, making her take her attention off me. When she pulled up in the driveway, he invited her in to meet his parents. She hesitated at first, but I knew her worry for me would compel her to check on things. Cade's mom was already on the porch, gesturing for us to come in by the time we got of the car. A little yellow VW Bug pulled up at the curb as we entered. I assumed it was Mouse's car.

"Hey, you two!" his mom exclaimed. "My Cade has told me so much about you. You must be Ember?" Without waiting for an answer, she pulled me into a hug. "I'm Catherine Malone, but please call me Cathy. And you're Kim?" she asked my mom.

"Yes, I'm Kim Watson. I'm sorry to impose, but…" "Oh, don't be ridiculous! Dave is still out at the car lot. I would love the company. Why don't we get a snack while the kids swim? Cade tells me you just moved in and are about to start redecorating. That's my specialty. No, I don't get paid for it…" Mrs. Malone's voice faded as she herded mom into the kitchen.

"I'm sorry," said Cade. "She's very…exuberant."

"I like her," I said honestly. He gestured behind me, and I turned to see Mouse come in the glass door.

"Why don't you two use my sister's old room to get dressed? Mouse knows where it is. I'm going to find out what's going on with my truck first. I'll meet you out back soon." He turned toward the kitchen, and I felt a little bit of panic. I don't know if it was because he left me alone with Mouse or just because he left me. It was a scary thought.

"This way," she said, interrupting my thoughts. With one last look toward the kitchen, I followed her upstairs.

She showed me to a pretty room on the right side of the hall and gestured toward the bathroom. I changed into my swimsuit and wrapped up in a towel. When I came out, Mouse was already dressed in her swimsuit and white terry cover-up, sitting on the edge of the bed. I stood there for a minute, but she didn't attempt to move, so I sat down beside her.

"It's not so much that I'm shy as it is…I just usually regret what I say after I've said it. I've learned to keep my mouth shut; that way I don't have to keep myself up at night replaying and cringing at every word." The words tumbled out as if Mouse knew she would stop them if she paused to take a breath.

I really didn't have a clue of what to say to such a strange confession, so instead I changed the subject. "Cade calls you 'Mouse,' but that can't be your real name, can it?" I asked, suddenly unsure.

"It's Melissa. I'm Melissa," she answered. "First, my nickname was 'Missy,' then somewhere along the way it evolved to 'Mini,' then, 'Minnie Mouse,' and finally, I just became 'Mouse.'"

"Do you mind?" I asked.

"I guess it's better than being named after a Disney character," she said with a chuckle. "And, considering my size and demeanor, it fits; so no, I don't mind so much. Not anymore. Cade says you're a Christian," Missy declared in an abrupt change of subject.

"Yeah, I am. I mean I think so. No. Of course, I am," I said, confusing even myself.

"I don't like to talk much," Missy said, and added, "but I'm a great listener."

I found her to be spot-on, because for the next few minutes I told her about my life while she encouraged me with nods of encouragement and rapt attention. I told her about my childhood of poverty, salvation at twelve, the life of wealth and excess I lived for the next four years (although I skimmed over a lot of the worst details), and how I ended up here.

When I finished she declared, "You're still a Christian, Ember. You're just loaded down by the mistakes you've made. God still loves you. He always will. Will you go with me to my church's teen group tomorrow night?" she asked abruptly.

I still felt the aftershock of her declaration, so it took me a minute to respond. A smile crept over my face as I felt a familiar hope; a hope that the separation I'd felt for so long wasn't a life sentence after all. "Yeah, I'd love to go," I said and meant it.

By the time we came downstairs, the house was quiet and empty so we followed the sound of "Blackfoot" out to the pool. Cade had already been swimming. He was standing on the diving board about to jump when he saw us. Seeing him there, grinning at me, took my breath away.

"It's about time!" he yelled, just before making a perfect dive.

I took advantage of his being underwater and quickly shed my towel and jumped, feet first, into the shallow end. That was a big mistake; talk about taking away breath! The cold water was a painful shock to my system. Cade popped out of the water beside me and sang along with the group, something about leaving and being a hobo. I just laughed and tried to avoid being splashed. Missy joined us (I refused to call her Mouse anymore) and soon we were all swimming and singing along to Cade's endless Southern rock playlist.

Not until I got out for a bathroom break did I notice my mom was still there. I stood there drying off, amazed at what I saw. She was sitting at the table with Cade's mother under the shade of an oak tree, laughing so hard tears were running down her face. She unwittingly reached over and scratched their dog.

In spite of weighing more than her, Raven tried to climb on Mom's lap, which made both women laugh even harder. I realized that for the first time in a long time, she was being herself and truly having a great time. Mom must have felt me looking at her because she patted her face with a napkin and looked at me. In that moment, I knew she recognized the same thing in herself. She gave me a little nod and smile and I jogged on to the bathroom. When I came out, a man, who I assumed was Cade's father, was standing at the counter opening some kind of liquor bottle. I made it as far as the sliding glass door before he discovered me.

"Hey," he said, "you must be a friend of Cade's." He said something under his breath I didn't catch, and then stuck out his hand for me to shake.

"Yes, sir" I replied and shook his hand.

He held it there just a little too long. It was almost imperceptible, but it still made me uncomfortable; or maybe it was how he smiled at me. Cade had looked at me before in a way that made me feel pretty. Although this man had the same blue eyes, they made me feel slimy instead. I pulled my hand away immediately, closed my towel tighter around me, and took a step back to the door. I almost fell through when Cade opened it.

He steadied me and joked, "We thought you got lost. Hi, Dad," he said cheerfully when he noticed his father.

Cade moved in front of me, blocking his dad's view. I don't think he realized what he had done; then again, maybe I was just imagining things.

"Mom told me my truck would be ready tomorrow," he continued. His dad took one last, futile glance in my direction then went back to making his drink.

"Yeah, they had to get it delivered from a dealer in Alabama. I think you'll really like it."

Anderson Public Library
Lawrenceburg, KY 40342

They started talking shop, so I made my exit. Mom waved me over and asked if everything was OK. Missy had joined them and also looked concerned.

"Yeah, I'm fine," I lied. "I was just talking to Mr. Malone."

Cade's mom looked at her watch and exclaimed, "Oh my, is it that late already?"

Mom looked surprised too and started talking about leaving. Missy didn't bother with goodbyes. She was already walking toward the side of the house. I ran to catch up with her.

"What about your clothes?" I asked.

"Cade will know to drop them by the restaurant when he gets a chance. Will I see you at the teen group tomorrow night?" she asked, getting into her car. She rolled down the window so I could speak to her through the passenger seat.

"Yeah, I'm looking forward to it," I said.

She rewarded me with a huge smile. I backed up and waved as she pulled away from the curb. Mom was saying goodbye to the Malones on the front porch. Cade jogged to me with my backpack and Missy's bag in his arms.

"I can't believe the day is already over," he said. "It was amazing."

I agreed. Mom called for me from the car.

"I'd better go," I said grudgingly and took the bags from him. "Talk to you tomorrow?" I asked.

"No," he said with a dramatic pause, then continued with a mischievous smile. "Tonight."

I willed my legs to move and hummed "Free Bird" as I made my way to the car.

That night I lay in my bed after a long conversation with Cade, and thought about my mom's concerned look in the car that day. I thought about how attached I already felt to him. I'd

had boyfriends before, but I had never felt this way about any of them. As I replayed their faces in my mind, I slowly began to realize why their memories didn't make me have any kind of emotional response. Those guys were chosen for me by the "plastics" on their quest to mold me into another version of them. I was just a challenge for them. They picked the popular, handsome guys, the ones as shallow as themselves, and set me up. I went along with it, of course, the ever-changing chameleon that I was. I had never truly liked any of them. Cade was the first one who I had fallen for without any outside prodding or pressure. I guessed my mother wasn't the only one suffering from an identity crisis. No wonder I had felt such empathy toward her yesterday. That insight, and the hope of Missy's words, brought me comfort in knowing that it might be possible for me to become that person who I thought had been lost, the "real me."

Chapter Three

I WOKE UP, FRANTICALLY looking around the room. The walls were still there and sunlight was streaming in through my still undressed window. I swiped my hair, wet with sweat and tears, from my face and waited for the remnants of unease associated with the nightmare to fade. The smell of bacon brought me fully back to reality. I threw my legs over the bed, slipped on my bedroom shoes, and followed my nose.

Mom had already set the table for breakfast and was sliding an omelet onto my plate, making my stomach growl with hunger I didn't realize was there.

"A pizza omelet?" I asked hopefully. Yesterday evening, I had been starving from swimming, so Mom and I picked up a pizza with everything and brought it home to eat with a movie. I took a bite before she could answer and found it loaded with all of the toppings from last night's leftovers. Delicious. "What's the occasion?" I asked between bites. I hadn't had my favorite breakfast since my fifteenth birthday.

"I'm sorry I missed your sixteenth birthday, honey. I hope you can forgive me. We never got your license or a car," she said, chewing her lip.

"It's no big deal. I had a fun time at the beach," I reassured her. In truth, I had wasted the time partying and hanging out with my cousin. I wondered if they had a car in mind before I left, or if they just forgot about my birthday completely.

"Well, I don't know when I'll have the chance to cook breakfast for you for a while," she said, interrupting my dark thoughts. "I start my new job at the clinic tomorrow, and I'm going to be busy on weekends working on the house. Will you be OK here by yourself while I'm at work?"

I had two new friends now, and I was getting tired of crawling over boxes to get to my bedroom door, so I would have plenty to do. "Yeah, it's not long until school," I answered. A text from Cade kept me from continuing. He wanted to take me for a drive in his new truck.

One look at Mom's face made me text back: *Not now. With Mom. Will call soon.*

Just as I dreaded, she inquired, "How are things going with Cade? You seem to be getting serious quickly."

"It's not what you think, Mom. I just like being around him. I feel like I can be myself again and that's good enough for him," I answered thoughtfully.

"Yes, I can tell you're definitely good enough for him," she said with a knowing smile. "Just let me know if you think it's starting to get very serious."

I knew what she meant. Mom was a nurse, after all. We'd had plenty of "talks" before. I was going to get defensive, but decided to take the easy road. I just nodded instead. That seemed to satisfy her and, thankfully, the conversation turned to lighter subjects. We chatted over the remainder of breakfast. While we were cleaning up the kitchen, she asked if I was still having nightmares.

"Yeah, I had one last night, but I think I know how to make them stop."

She dried the dishwater from her hands and leaned on the cabinet, ready to hear more. Instead, I said, "Which reminds me, Missy invited me to her church's teen group at seven tonight. Can you take me? She can probably drive me home."

"Sure," replied Mom. "I guess you haven't been involved in church since Rose used to take you as a kid."

Mrs. Rose Denton worked as a nurse at the hospital with mom and was also a single mom. She always had Sundays off, so I would tag along each week when she and her daughter, Violet, went to Sunday school. I asked Mom if she had heard from them lately. She told me she intended to email them, once we got Internet. Our time ended when I received another text. I didn't even bother reading it.

"It's probably Cade again, dying to show off his new truck. Mind if I go?" I asked.

"I guess its OK...," she began. I could tell there was more to come, so I tried to make a quick exit. She caught me before I made it to the hall. "Just be home right after lunch, Ember. We have a lot of work to do."

I sighed dramatically and went in my room to dig through boxes for the perfect outfit.

An hour or two later, I twirled around in front of my mirror to check out the results. I had taken extra care, giving myself a mini-facial and French manicure. I wore a cute navy blue strapless romper with strappy sandals. I heard a horn so I ran through the kitchen to give Mom a quick peck on the cheek. I had to slow down enough to listen to instructions about being careful before taking off again through the laundry room. When I walked out on the carport, I could see Cade through his windshield. He was wearing dark shades so I could only see teeth, which brought back memories of a certain Cheshire cat. The object of his glee was a new, screaming yellow, four-wheel drive, extended cab, Chevy truck. My date jumped out and ran around the passenger door. Cade gave a little bow and gave me a hand up. He looked extremely handsome. I could tell by his smile that he was having similar thoughts about me. I think he said something to that effect, but I couldn't hear him over Molly Hatchet's "Flirtin' With Disaster."

"Not a warning, I hope!" I yelled, pointing to the stereo.

Three tries later, he finally heard me, but only winked and took off down the road. I cringed when I thought about the possibility of Mom watching out the window, but his excitement was contagious. I joined in singing to the top of my lungs as we peeled off the highway and onto a dirt road leading into the woods. I didn't think to ask where we were going. He wouldn't have understood my question, anyway. Besides, it was nice not to care.

About five songs later, the woods cleared, opening up to a small pond. Cade drove slowly, but we still bounced in our seats as he drove around to the far side. He parked under a huge oak tree and got out. I waited for him to open my door then I commented on how beautiful it was there.

"You ain't seen nothin' yet," he joked as he walked to the back of the truck. I started to follow but he insisted I wait for him. I turned around and took in the beauty of the place. There were a few ducks swimming in our direction, but other than poultry, we were alone. The quiet sounds of nature seemed even more distinct after half an hour of electric guitar riffs. I walked to the edge of the water, took off my sandals and sunk my feet into the cool sand. Cade walked up behind me, putting his hands on my sides. After a minute, he eased me back toward him, circling his arms loosely around my waist into a hug. I leaned my back onto his chest, enjoying the feeling of his cheek against mine. He reached up and gently moved my hair to my other shoulder. He softly touched his lips to my neck, sending shocks through my body. I closed my eyes and enjoyed the feel of having him so close.

"Ember," he whispered. I slowly turned around to face him, not wanting to break the connection. I moved my hands up around his neck, running his soft, blond hair through my fingers. He looked down at me with tenderness and tightened his hold around my waist. "I know it's soon, but...I really like you, Ember," he confessed in a whisper then closed his eyes and lowered his mouth onto mine.

He kissed me gently, and then pulled back with a timid smile. A smile that was impossible not to return. I dropped my hands and took his from my waist. I held on, looking down at my wet feet, trying to put my feelings into words. Cade saved me from the difficult task. "You don't have to say anything. I told you I knew it was too soon." He balanced me as I put my sandals back on, and we walked hand in hand back up the bank to the oak tree.

When we neared the truck, he got behind me and covered my eyes with his hands. I laughed and went along with the game. We moved forward a few steps like that, almost tripping on a root. He whispered "surprise" in my ear and dropped his hands to my shoulders. Under the shade of the oak, he had arranged a red-checkered blanket with a huge picnic basket, overflowing with food, drinks, glasses, and utensils. The windows were down in the truck so his stereo could serenade us with love songs. I looked at him, rightly impressed.

"I would like to take all of the credit, but Mouse helped me out," he confessed with a shrug.

He looked so cute and insecure that I boldly responded by pulling his head down to mine in another kiss. As our feelings intensified, we lowered ourselves down to sit on the blanket. After a couple of minutes, I felt Cade guiding us back so we could lie down. The movement brought me back to my senses, so I resisted against the light pressure. He stopped immediately and we separated, both with shortness of breath and pounding hearts. I scooted away from him and straightened my hair a bit.

"So what kind of goodies did you bring us?" I asked trying to create a calm I didn't feel.

His voice came out in a croak, so he cleared it and tried again. "I'm not sure, but I told Mouse we wanted 'the works.'"

We leaned over the basket and grinned at each other in awe of the overabundance of food, or maybe it was because of what we had just shared together.

Later, we pulled up at my house stuffed and happy. I thanked Cade, and his awesome new truck, which he named—another stretch—Sunny. He walked around and helped me out. We stood there with the door open, leaning against the seat, his hands on my waist.

"I'm not ready to give you up so soon."

I started to remind him that I had promised to help Mom with the house, but he reached down and gave me a quick kiss before I could make excuses.

"I know you promised your mom an afternoon, but you're mine tonight."

He reached up and moved my hair behind my ear, obviously wanting a reason to touch me again.

"It's Sunday," I said.

I was met with a blank stare. I rolled my eyes but reminded him anyway. "I'm going to teen group with Missy tonight, but we can still be together. You can come with us."

He stepped back and put his hand on the door. "Nah, you two go enjoy some girl time."

I didn't know if I should be hurt by Cade's refusal to go with me or relieved that he wasn't the obsessive type. Confused, I stepped away from the truck as he got back in and rolled down the window. "You're off the hook tonight, but tomorrow I'm going to be over bright and early. Mouse and your mom will be at work, so no excuses!"

He backed the truck out of the driveway and gave me a smile as he pulled away. I decided to be happy.

I changed into a t-shirt and shorts right away, then reported for duty in the living room. Mom had already put one coat of paint on before I got home. It took two more coats, four hours, and her complete nineties playlist, but we finally had a nice light grey living room, just a shade darker than our furniture. We only got the chance to enjoy our hard work for a minute during a water break, then Mom got her second wind.

The small bedroom on the left after mine was designated as our office. It had yet to have anything done to it, so we attacked it next. The walls and carpet were beige and were both in fairly good shape, so Mom decided we could skip giving it a make-over and just organize and accessorize instead. We spent the next hour dusting, vacuuming, and shelving books while chatting about all the changes, good and bad, in our lives. We kept it light, and away from the subject of Cade, until Mom couldn't take it anymore.

"So, how was your date?" she began.

I knew she was just warming up. Normally, I wouldn't mind Mom asking me personal questions, but it touched a nerve for some reason. In spite of the irritation I felt, I decided to keep it nice. I told her all about his new truck, the drive, the pond, and the picnic.

"You wouldn't believe all of the food. I don't think I will ever be able to eat fried chicken again, even if it was the most delicious chicken I have ever tasted."

"And the kiss?" she asked from under the desk, plugging in computer wires.

"It was amazing...Hey! How did you know?" I asked, incredulous.

Mom backed out, careful not to bump her head. She sat down in our brown leather desk chair with a sigh. "Sweetie, you have been distracted from the moment you came in the door."

I didn't think I had been acting preoccupied. I guess it was just a "Mom-radar" thing she has going for her sometimes.

"Did it get out of hand?" she hedged.

"Absolutely not," I promised. "It could have, I guess, but I put on the brakes. We stopped *way* before it got intense, and he was a perfect gentleman about it," I stressed to drive home my point.

"Then, why so glum?" I looked at her confused. How was she picking up on those vibes?

"I'm not glum about Cade; I'm just confused. I feel great when I'm with him, but when I'm not, that same feeling comes back. It's hollowness or something. I can't describe it."

I couldn't. I just knew there had to be more to life than parties, new cars, clothes, and boyfriends. I had definitely tried to fill the void with those things over the last four years, but it still felt like I had a gaping hole inside of me. Even the biggest skeptic would have no choice but to believe my theory. You would think I could get it through my own thick skull. Instead, I finally got a chance at a fresh start and I seemed to be going off the same cliff.

"I'm doing an awful job of understanding myself at all lately," I added, frustrated. Mom moved off the chair to sit on the floor.

She leaned against the bookcase and stared up at the ceiling, probably wondering how she landed such a weird kid.

"Honey, I think you and Cade are just moving a little too fast." For someone so intuitive, she missed the mark by a mile. Yes, we were moving too fast. I had already promised myself I wouldn't have another boyfriend until college, but that wasn't the point and I didn't know how to get it across, so I just nodded instead.

"Yeah, you're right. I shouldn't have let him kiss me, especially on our first date." Mom laughed at that.

"As many hours as you guys have spent together and on the phone, I don't think today would qualify as a first date. I do think you should give yourselves a little breathing room. Missy seems like a nice girl. Maybe you two could hang out more. Hey, would you like to invite her to sleep over one night?"

I jumped up and looked at the desk clock.

"Oh no, I've got to get a shower! Teen group starts in an hour, and I'm not even sure how to find the church!"

Mom didn't seem to share my panic. Instead, she slowly stood up and stretched out her back.

"I met her parents today when I stopped by their restaurant for lunch. Why don't you get ready and I'll look them up and give them a call for the address? I can put it in the GPS."

She sighed and began looking under stacks of paperwork for the phone book.

"It would be so much easier if our Internet was up. Thankfully, a guy will be by tomorrow."

I nodded, quickly adding the last few books to the shelf, and left her to her search.

Deciding what to wear was harder than usual. Most of the memories of attending church were of wearing ruffled dresses, white tights, and black patent shoes. It looked like Macy's had exploded by the time I finished, but I was finally satisfied with my choice of an emerald green silk shirtdress with the compulsory ruffles down the front. I didn't own any hose and hoped that my legs were tanned enough that it wouldn't be noticeable. I added extra lotion on my knees, just in case, and slipped on my sling back Louboutin pumps. They were black and shiny like the shoes of my childhood but the four-and-a-half-inch heels and red soles made them all grown up. After one last glance in the mirror for a makeup check, I made my way through piles of discarded clothes as I went out to catch my ride.

It was just getting dark as we pulled up in front of the church. It looked deserted, so Mom circled the extensive grounds until we saw signs of life in the back of one of the buildings. There were a couple dozen cars in the parking lot and about twice as many teens milling around.

"Looks like we've found the place," I observed and suddenly began feeling nervous.

It occurred to me that although I had lived in this town for a few days, I had always had Cade with me to show me around. I had never felt like the "new girl" until now. Mom noticed my unease and patted my knee.

"Maybe it's a good thing to get this over with now. By the time you start school, you'll have lots of friends."

She moved the car forward and parked next to the curb. I hesitated before getting out, scanning the area for all possible exits. A sidewalk ran perpendicularly to the car. Just beyond, in a grassy area, there was a handsome, black-haired teen tossing a football to some other guys. The scene from *The Brady Bunch* rerun where Marsha got whacked in the face with a football came to mind, but I squelched the memory. I could see that walking past the guys was inevitable. The short set of steps leading to the entrance was just beyond. Lights streamed from the glass doors. Suddenly, I was the scared little twelve-year-old girl again, being ripped from my world of familiar poverty. With one last glance back at Mom, I drew a shaky breath and stepped out toward the unknown. Nothing could have prepared me for reality.

I nervously tugged on my mini-dress to keep from flashing anyone. By the time I looked up from smoothing and pulling, I was surrounded by teens. I gave a panicked look back toward Mom, but all I could make out was the Mercedes' taillights in the distance. I wanted to play a lost tourist and walk away, pretending I wasn't just left by my ride. I nervously tucked my hair behind my ear and smiled instead. My "I bring you no harm" look must have done the trick because I was instantly flooded with hands extended in greeting and what sounded like names being thrown in my direction. Relief spread over me and I made a slow circle around the group that had surrounded me, trying to put names with faces, knowing if put to the test I would fail miserably. The girls were asking about my clothes, while the guys were making jokes and giving a stab at small talk. It was overwhelming, but somehow my old training kicked in. I turned up my smile and began chatting with the guys and giggling with the girls. Thankfully, through a gap in the crowd, I saw a familiar face standing on the steps.

"Missy!" I exclaimed and waved at her. She must have not seen me because she turned around and started toward the door. "Wait up!" I yelled to her as I made my way through my impromptu welcoming party and up the stairs.

I caught up with her right as she walked in the church. The room was very large, close to the size of a school gym, but was carpeted with the blue indoor/outdoor variety. The walls looked like large concrete blocks disguised by pale yellow paint, reminding me of a skating rink I had occasionally visited as a kid. Four or five rows of plastic blue chairs lined each side of us as we entered. The facing wall had the same setup, facing us. There was a small rounded stage minus the curtains to the left, with various instruments poised for play. A lone musician sat on a high wooden stool strumming a guitar, lost in a tune that only the two of them could hear. Across the room, on the far right corner, was a half wall—another reminder of a rink—that corralled what seemed to be video games; if the flashing lights, dinging sounds, and yelps of teens were any indication.

My gaze was drawn away from the games when I noticed Missy had walked away to a door to the right of us. I couldn't catch up, something I thought was both amusing and frustrating since her legs were so much shorter than mine were and she didn't have that much of a head start. I was close enough behind her to catch the smell of popcorn wafting through the door as she opened it. The smell made my mouth water, but not in a good way. I guess I was still more nervous than I would have liked to admit. I took a few more steps in and even more smells attacked my senses. We were in a long, wide hall that housed some type of concession stand but resembled a coffee shop more. To my left was a long counter displaying a selection of baked goodies, coffee and food condiments, and fountain drinks.

Two middle-aged women waved at Missy from behind the station. A large section of wall to the right was glass. Inside were a few tables, mostly empty except for one. Two pretty girls my age were sitting together smiling up at a group of admiring guys vying for their attention. One guy glanced my way, attracting the attention of the whole group. I stood there wide-eyed for a second, empathizing with zoo animals, when Missy took my arm and led me to a restroom, just past the food court. The restroom had a separate sitting area, so we plopped down on the sofa in unison. I hoped she could make me understand why I attracted all those people like bugs to a light.

"Why was I mobbed?"

"You really don't know do you?" she asked, shaking her head in disbelief. "You pull up in a Mercedes-Benz, S-class, no less. You're dressed to the nines in designer clothes and stilettos that probably cost more than most of these kids make in a month at their fast food jobs and you don't understand why you would attract attention?"

I didn't like what her tone insinuated. No, I didn't like what her tone accused. I was hurt and angry, so I took the only action I could think of at the time; I got up to leave. Missy stopped me by grabbing my arm before I could reach the door.

"Mouse," indeed, I thought with a huff.

I stopped but glared, with laser beam eyes, at her hand that still gripped my arm. She took the hint and dropped it with a sigh.

"I'm sorry. I wanted to believe you weren't just showing off, but just look at you," she demanded, giving a dramatic sweep of her arm over the length of me that Vanna White would have envied.

I felt like my clothes had just been labeled "Exhibit A."

"It was a grand entrance that everyone will be talking about for days. Congratulations, Ember, you just landed yourself a 'get popular free' card," Missy said, making me more miserable with every word.

I sat back down on the sofa, knees together and head in hands. My desire to be normal and fit in had backfired miserably.

Instead, I managed to end up just like I was before—a plastic—and I didn't even have my old "friends" to blame for it, just myself. I felt the sofa move beside me as Missy sat down.

She tentatively put her arm around my shoulders. "Ember, I'm sorry. You told me that day at Cade's house how miserable you were in your last school. That's why I was so upset when I saw you tonight…acting that way. I thought that maybe you weren't being honest that day."

Her confession brought tears to my eyes. I started blubbering about trying to fit in, ruffles, and black, shiny shoes. I don't know if Missy could make out any of it through my hands that covered my face, but she acted like she did and kept tissues coming so I guess that's all that mattered. After I was cried out, I looked over at Missy and asked, "You know the real tragedy of this evening?" She shook her head no, so I continued, "You've said more to me in anger than you have in all our other conversations combined." She just smiled and passed me a peace offering, her makeup bag.

After I had cleaned up, I wanted to call my mom and get out of there. Missy insisted that I should stick with it, promising to stay by my side. I reluctantly accepted and, with bravado I didn't feel, walked out of the restroom. The smell of food accosted me again. This time it made my stomach rumble loudly with hunger instead of nausea. I felt like that was a good sign. Missy must have agreed because she gave me a smile and directed us to the food counter. She told me since I was a first-time visitor, I could have a free combo. I settled for some popcorn and lemonade, not trusting my stomach just yet. Missy opened her wallet and took out something that looked like Monopoly money but had their church's logo on it.

"We get church bucks for our volunteer work around here. My family provides a steady stream of baked goods, so I'm loaded."

The women in the back smiled and nodded in agreement. It was almost time for the service to start and I didn't want to be the last one to enter. Missy insisted that eating in the big room was allowed.

"Is it a gym or theater?" I asked as we grabbed some napkins and straws before going in.

"Neither," she replied. "It's just the teen room. The gym is at the other end of the hall. Our theater is next door."

I was impressed and concluded that the whole town must attend here, though I knew I had seen other churches. My thoughts abruptly ended when she opened the door and dozens of sets of eyeballs all turned in our direction. I stayed behind Missy, though she was too small to act as much of a shield. Thankfully, she felt my pain and led us over to the closest chairs; or maybe she was tired of me grabbing the back of her shirt and stepping on her heels.

Much to my relief, the moment passed quickly as a man who looked to be close to my mother's age grabbed a little wooden podium and set it down in front of the group with a thud. He had a short, military cut, but that's where the straight-laced look ended. He wore cut-offs, a t-shirt that looked like a drink ad, but I think had Christian connotations, and flip-flops. He leaned on the stand for a minute with a big grin, taking us all in, then pulled his cell phone out of his pocket, held it up, and silenced it. Suddenly, there was a lot of commotion in the room as we all followed suit. While waiting for everyone to comply, he greeted a couple of people, then he noticed me. I slid down in my seat a little, dreading the inevitable introduction request, and was pleasantly surprised as he continued to peruse the crowd, ignoring me.

"Well, it's great to see all of the familiar faces, and the new ones," he added, looking pointedly at me.

So he did notice me, but didn't rat me out. I liked this guy already.

"For those of you who are here for the first time, or who just really suck at names" (he got a few laughs out of that), "I am the youth pastor here and my name is Eric. All of you can call me Pastor Eric."

He spent a few minutes talking a little about himself and the group, all for my benefit I'm sure. The jokes were for everyone.

After the short introduction, Pastor Eric grabbed a Bible off an empty seat in front of him. He could have had his pick of spots; the front row was barren except for the random tip of a shoe that peeked through the back of the seat. He flipped open to a spot saved by a bulletin, nodded to show he had found what he was looking for, and, without hesitation, broke into prayer. I dropped my head as quickly as I realized he was talking to God instead of us, but still missed it by a few seconds.

"Dear God, we have come here tonight…"

My mind started to recap earlier events, but I only got up to opening the car door and he was finished, short and sweet. His message was short too, but it rocked my world nonetheless. Pastor Eric's message was titled, "When Pigs Fly." It was based on a story from the Bible about the prodigal son. I was surprised to realize that I still remembered the story from my early years in Sunday school. Honestly, I think it was the visual of a guy eating slop with pigs that made it stick. By the time Pastor Eric finished, I knew the message was directly aimed at me, though I was positive he couldn't have planned it that way. I also knew that I was just like the prodigal son and, most importantly, my Father still loved me. He was waiting with open arms, and I was more than ready to be clean and free of my past sins.

Although Pastor Eric's message was short, I was on pins and

needles by the time he finished. I wanted him to pray with me. I didn't have one thought about my clothes, shoes, or mascara-stained face. He passed around handouts with chapters and verses that went deeper into the lesson and then closed.

"If any of you have sins that are weighing down on you, all you have to do is ask for Jesus to forgive you, and He will. Let's have a silent prayer."

I didn't even try to bow my head that time. I just looked at the top of his in disbelief. I distinctly remembered some sweet lady holding my hand and praying with me when I got saved at my last church. I guess here, you're just expected to wing it. Maybe Missy was right, and I was still a Christian; a really lousy one, but maybe it would be easier this time to confess my sins. They weren't going to stay silent forever, so I ducked my head and silently gave a quick rundown of as many sins as I could remember and finished off the list with "and anything else that was wrong," just in case. I didn't feel much of anything until I added, with complete conviction, "I'm so sorry for forgetting You, Jesus. Please forgive me. I know I'm just me, a mixed up teenager who screws up a lot, but You made me, so I can't be that bad. I know You had a reason for putting me here because I want to do more than just go to heaven. I want to help change the earth." I shuddered when I thought about my nightmare. "Help me make a difference, for You." I didn't know where the last part came from; I had intended just to make good with the Big Guy. Wherever it came from, I had meant it with every fiber of my being. For once in my life, I was happy, even excited, just to be me.

When I looked up, I noticed some others had already finished and were talking quietly. I guess Pastor Eric was keeping them reined in because he saw I was still praying. I was a little embarrassed, but mostly relieved because of the lightness I felt in my chest. It was a feeling I had forgotten existed and a peace I didn't realize I was without until now. Missy and I both looked at each other. I nodded my head at her silent question and returned her smile through tears of joy.

As if on cue, the volume picked up and Pastor Eric came over for an introduction. He seemed genuinely happy to have me there and extended the invitation to come back anytime. After I thanked him, there was a pregnant silence. Finally, he asked nervously, "Did you make any decisions tonight?" Decisions? To attend? I was sure he was speaking church-ese, but I racked my brain and came up blank. Once again, Missy saved the day.

"She rededicated."

She had obviously said the right thing because he grinned, shook my hand heartedly, and breathed, "Wonderful" and all of its synonyms at least twice.

Some girl came over and reminded him about the time, but not before giving me the stink eye behind Pastor Eric's back; funny thing is, it didn't bother me one bit. I may not fit in on the outside, but the on the inside…I was good to go. It was an exhilarating feeling.

Everyone must have caught on to my renewed confidence, or maybe it was Missy's warning glares, because I didn't get any bad or extremely flirtatious vibes from anyone the rest of the evening. In fact, I had a lot of fun.

It started with Pastor declaring it was time for team-building exercises. We participated in all kinds of fun races that you would normally see at a seven year old's birthday party (I took off my heels for those). Later, we caught each other as we fell from the side of the stage in something that resembled crowd surfing in a spiritual mosh pit. After, everyone chatted over fountain drinks in the café; then we divided into creative teams to plan the back to school party scheduled for August. Everyone was a little stressed about having enough time. There were only three more teen meetings until the big event. Finally, we had "free play" in the gym. It basically consisted of guys trying to look cool while trying to steal a ball from an opponent and getting it into some type of net while the girls worked hard on pretending not to notice. Some things don't change no matter what the zip code.

Missy drove me home and we made the pleasant discovery, though not surprising considering the size of the town, that she lived only a few streets down from me. Our mostly one-sided conversation during the drive didn't feel strained at all. In fact, I think I was able to convey how much fun I had and even how different I felt since praying. She managed to be very silently supportive. I steered clear of talking about the spat we had before the meeting, except to say I would know to dress more comfortably next time. The old me would have asked her where to buy clothes that would help me blend into the crowd. The transformed one decided that, beyond donating my secret stash of party clothes, I was keeping what I already owned. I was tired of being a chameleon, changing colors every time I ended up with a new group. I know it sounded cliché, but it's what's on the inside that counts. And I was certain of who was on the inside.

Missy pulled up at my house by 10:30 with the promise to visit after work one day that week. Only the porch light was on, so I assumed Mom was already in bed. She had to be exhausted from all of the work on the house and from the thought of returning to work for the first time in over four years. I let myself in and got ready for bed. I was tired myself, but wanted to check out something from earlier today. I tiptoed down the hall to the office and turned on the small desk light. Mom's room was across the hall, but her door was closed, so chances were slim that she would wake up. I peered around the room to find it completely clean and organized. She had obviously put in some extra time after she dropped me off at church. I felt a little guilty, but decided I would make it up to her this week. I would have plenty of time while she was at work to fix things up, especially my room, which was becoming close to unlivable. If I didn't take action soon, I might just disappear in there one day.

I walked over to the shelf I had begun organizing earlier and searched until I found what I was looking for. There, tucked away in the shelves along with the non-fiction, was Mom's old Bible. I hugged it to myself and decided to keep it for a while. She wouldn't mind. I had never even seen her open it; besides, although I had two Bibles, one that Mrs. Denton had given to me for my eighth birthday and the white one on my memory shelf, one was small and was missing a testament, and the other had illustrations.

I turned off the light and padded back down the hall to my room, treasure in tow. I was excited to read the companion scriptures Pastor Eric had given us that night, so I dug out a booklight and crawled into bed. That evening in my room was a night of firsts for me. It was the first time I had ever fallen asleep sitting up with a Bible in my lap. It was also the first time my phone had stayed on "silent" and remained uncharged throughout the night.

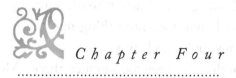

Chapter Four

MONDAY MORNING, I woke up with a crick in my neck, drool on my cheek and shaken to the core from yet another nightmare; not the best way to greet the day. I wiped my mouth with my sheet and tried to turn my head all the way to the side, to no avail. I did manage to twist it far enough to notice that I hadn't even cracked open Mom's Bible last night—so much for dedication.

I shuffled my way into the kitchen, deciding some sunny Florida orange juice would lift my spirits. There was none; only some kind of orange juice wannabe. I slammed the refrigerator in frustration, causing a spasm of pain to shoot down my neck. I reached out a fist to give the stupid refrigerator the what for, when I noticed Mom had stuck a note on it. It was a "to do" list for the day.

"And a great day to you too, Mom," I replied bitterly to the paper.

There went my great idea of surprising her with a clean house. Now, she just expected it; which ruined all the fun. With a huff, I stormed over to the sink to get some water. A plate of brownies distracted me off my path. Mom liked to cook, but would never bake anything. When I had to participate in bake sales, I always took pre-packaged cookies; embarrassing, but true. My instincts proved correct when I inspected the platter and discovered it wasn't ours. A friendly neighborhood visitor must have brought them while I was gone. I knew it would hurt my neck to put it back down so I took the entire thing into the living room prepared to eat my foul mood away.

I was shoveling in brownie number three (Mom definitely didn't make them, they were delicious), when I saw a yellow flash pass by the front of the house. In a panic, I jumped up, yelled in pain, and took off running to my room. A few minutes passed so I decided my peripheral vision wasn't all that, which didn't bode well for me and my stiff neck, and came out of hiding. I was walking into the front hallway on the way back to my waiting platter of brownies when I saw the eyes looking in through the triangle-shaped glass on the front door. Blue eyes.

I was tired of running, so I snatched open the door and whispered vehemently, "What are you doing here?"

When I saw the shock on Cade's face, my first thought was that I might have been a little too disagreeable. When the look remained frozen like that, I looked down at myself. I was in my usual sleep ensemble, t-shirt and boxers, but they were stained with chocolate. A hand rubbed across my mouth came back brown and slimy. I didn't even want to think about my teeth. I slammed the door and yelled, "Go away, Mom's not home!" through the door.

"I'm not going anywhere until I find out why you're avoiding me," he shouted back with equal determination.

I think he said something about my not being able to scare him away. Hopefully, he was talking about my intimidating presence, not my appearance. Either way, Cade had picked the wrong day to show off his stubborn streak, poor guy. I just shrugged and left him standing outside while I made my way to the bathroom to clean up.

Thirty minutes, a shower of blistering hot water, and a handful of Icy Hot later, I felt human again. I threw on some sweatshorts and an oyster bar t-shirt, then decided to hide the brownies out of my sight before I did more damage. I almost dropped the platter when I looked up and saw Cade staring at me through the living room window. I stomped over, threw open the door, making him jump, and yelled at him again. He wasn't supposed to be there while my mother was gone. (Why did I feel like I was in a Dr. Seuss book?) I feared it was too late, though. Half of the town had probably already noticed the fluorescent truck in the driveway and his "love in" on my front porch.

He looked at me calmly and then had the audacity to ask me to do the same. "Ember, you didn't return any of my texts or calls yesterday or this morning. I was worried."

I chewed my bottom lip as I tried to think of the last time I had talked to him on the phone.

"I'm serious. I've been trying to reach you for ages. Go check your phone."

I looked at him skeptically, but motioned for him to come in, with the strict instructions to wait in the hallway. I looked around my bedroom but didn't see my phone anywhere, which wasn't surprising considering the mess. Where did I have it last? Church! I picked up the green dress I had worn the night before and dug in the pocket. "That's hot. You sure you went to church?" he quipped from my doorway.

I turned around, startled. "I told you to wait in the hall!"

"I *am* in the hall," he smirked. "Besides, I brought you an important package that was lying there, undiscovered, on your front porch. I think it's your Internet modem. You owe me."

I just rolled my eyes and pulled out the phone, so he laid the box down by my door. "Look, Cade, I'm sorry about worrying you, but I obviously just forgot to turn up the ringer last night. It's no big deal," I said, suddenly feeling tired; probably the inevitable sugar crash from the brownie overload. My phone was dead so I plugged it into the charger and checked the volume. "Now you *really* need to go," I said over my shoulder. "Fine," he conceded. "When does your mom get home? I'll come over then."

I did *not* feeling like getting into a difficult discussion right then, but I couldn't see a way to avoid it.

"About that," I began, "we should probably slow down a little. You know, not see each other quite so much." I watched as confusion, then anger, flashed across his face. "Why? Because of *that*?" he accused, jabbing a finger toward my bed.

My gaze followed his to the Bible lying there. Now it was my time to be confused and angry. I didn't exactly know what he was getting at, nor did I care. I pushed past him and walked out of my room toward the front door. I had my hand on the doorknob when he walked up behind me.

"Ember, I thought we really had something special. I can't believe you're just going to toss it because they brainwashed you at church."

I spun around and shot daggers at him. "Cade Malone, my *mother* told me to slow things down, not anyone at church." I opened the door and waited for him to pass through. When he walked out onto the porch, I added, "and I totally agree with her," before closing the door and locking it.

I leaned up against the door, heart pounding in my chest, and waited. I didn't realize I was holding my breath until I heard the squeal of Cade's tires as he left. I stood there and contemplated what to do next; anything but cry or call for my "mommy," I concluded. I pushed away from the door and toward the one place I could lose myself, my trashed bedroom. I stopped at the doorway and forced myself to see the room through my mother's eyes; the unmade bed, discarded clothing strewn around the room, unpacked boxes against the walls, and my memory wall that hadn't been touched since Cade and I worked on it together. I felt tears stinging my eyes, so I quickly detoured away from that train of thought. I decided a basic pick up would be the best plan of attack. I would unpack boxes *after* I could see my floor.

I popped in my earphones, turned on my favorite playlist, named "Move It," and threw myself into the work with gusto. I took all my dirty clothes to the laundry room, where I discovered a box of hangers, so I picked up all my clean clothes and hung them neatly, by type and color, in my closet. All the shoes I had worn lately went on my shoe caddy. I organized my cosmetics in the small wicker baskets Mom had left under the bathroom sink. I was doing great, until I decided to take a break for lunch. When I turned off my iPod, the quietness of the house flooded me. The realization that I was completely alone, for the first time in a long time, hit me. I made myself a peanut butter and jelly sandwich, and ate in lonely silence. I walked back to my room, intending to get back to work, but my heart wasn't in it. Instead, I walked to my shelves and found the pendant Cade had left for me there. I held it in my hand and regretted how I had treated him. He was obviously just hurt that I had blown him off. It seemed like I was doing everything wrong lately. This new life was not turning out as I had hoped. Worse, I had that gnawing feeling inside me that said there was more, even to this life. I felt like I was just biding my time when everything was going to "hell in a handbasket" right outside the security of my bedroom. What was I missing? I thought rededicating my life to Christ would make me content, but instead I just felt more urgency to do *something*. Standing there in the middle of my room, I thought back to last night's dream and realized it was even more vivid.

Frustrated, I slammed the pendant back down on the shelf and walked over to make up my bed, set on purging out the endless questions and finishing the task. I grabbed my bedding, unexpectedly knocking Mom's Bible to the floor. I knelt to pick it up, but stayed there on my knees. I leaned over, head in my hands, and began to pray. I cried out to God, asking Him for help. I knelt there by my bed for a very long time, crying until all of my tears dried up. I sat up and slowly shifted from my knees to lean up against my bed. I reached over, grabbed the box of tissues off my nightstand and held it in my lap, waiting for my legs to wake up. Slowly, a smile crept across my face as I began to realize that I felt happy. It didn't make sense. Nothing had changed, except for a stuffy nose and stinging legs, but I knew that I could deal with things now. I knew I wasn't alone.

By the time Mom got home that evening, my room was immaculate and dinner was on the table. It was Chinese delivery, but food nonetheless. By the gaping "fish out of water" look she gave me upon seeing my room, I concluded that she was very impressed. She gave me a big hug and went to change out of her scrubs before we ate. I was pouring us iced tea when she came in and had a seat. I listened as she told me all about her first day. She would work as a receptionist in the clinic until she updated her nursing license, but still seemed genuinely happy to be working again, regardless of the position. Mom had gone through so much since I was born; the change I had seen in her the last few days made me happy and proud for her. I told her so. She bit her lip and had tears in her eyes. She reached across the table and took my hand.

"Ember, it has been hard, but everything I have gone through has been worth it; having you in my life has been my greatest joy." She let go of my hand and pushed her empty plate back. "I want you to be happy, too. That's why it's difficult for me to talk about this right now, but it has to be done."

I put down my fork and looked at her with confusion, bracing myself for the attack that I heard in her voice.

"Word got to me at work that Cade Malone's truck was parked in our driveway this morning. The person didn't see you two outside, so I have to assume that he was in our house; something that you know is wrong." Her voice got louder and firmer as she continued, "I don't have many rules, Ember, but you know having guys over without my presence, or at least my permission, is one that I strictly enforce."

"Mom...," I began.

"No, Ember. I don't want excuses. I don't want to hear 'nothing bad happened.' I just want you to answer a simple question with a 'yes' or 'no.' Were the two of you alone in this house this morning?"

I just sat there for a minute staring at my hands, trying to come up with a way out of this mess. I couldn't believe she wasn't even going to let me explain. She shut down any possible out with her "no excuses" move. I didn't see that one coming. Truth was I did let him in, knowing good and well someone would probably rat me out. Stupid town. They probably had moles assigned to scout around for juicy gossip. It's not like I even was excited to see him. Now, that was an interesting thought. Did I not want to see Cade or was I just in a lousy mood? I didn't get to answer myself because Mom interrupted my self-examination.

"Jacquelyn Ember Matthews, I'm waiting."

I knew I was in for it then. She never used my full name; it reminded her of Bio-dad too much. I grudgingly admitted, "Yes, he was here, but..." I made one last desperate attempt to argue my side, but it was not to be.

"There's nothing more I need to hear," she interrupted, then she handed down my sentence. "You will not leave this house, unless you are with me, for three weeks."

"*Three weeks*! That would only leave one week of freedom before school starts!" I shouted, jumping out of my chair. She just gave me a steely look. I had seen it before; she wasn't going to budge, so I tried a new tactic. "What about if I only hang out with Missy?"

She just shook her head stubbornly.

"That's ridiculous!" I huffed and I almost added, *Nothing happened with Cade...except a fight*, but angrily decided to keep quiet. I could have explained everything and put her mind at ease, but she refused to listen, so, let her wonder. I knew there was one thing she would feel too guilty to say no to.

"What about the teen group at church?"

She stood up and started clearing the dishes from the table. After a minute she responded, "I guess that's OK; as long as it's just the one night a week and I take you and pick you up."

It was a small victory, but I was still reeling from the unfairness of it all. "Do I get regular food during my jail time or just bread and water?" I asked defiantly. I couldn't help it. This was crazy. She had never cared before we moved here.

Mom turned and gave me a look that would have turned the most hardened criminal's heart to stone, so I made a quick retreat to my room to lick my wounds.

"That's the payback I get for all of my hard work," I mumbled to no one in particular.

I decided to protest Mom's unfairness by staying in my room for the rest of the evening. I wouldn't see her before she left for work in the morning either, giving her a full twenty-four hours to rethink her decision. I opened the Bible to read the scriptures Pastor Eric had given us, but found I wasn't in the mood to read about a disobedient child, so I closed it and prayed instead. I talked to God a long time about how wrong I was treated and asked Him to please help Mom see the error of her ways so I could have my life back. I sat there expectantly a few minutes, but didn't feel any of the peace I had felt earlier that day when I had prayed, so I decided to talk to someone else instead.

I called Missy and told her the horrible news about my restriction. I whined and ranted, but kept silent about the bit that Cade's visit caused the problem, though I wasn't quite sure why I would want to protect him. As usual, Missy didn't say much, but she did make sympathetic sounds in all the right places.

Two hours into my self-imposed lock down and I was going a little stir crazy, walking around in circles and biting my nails. If only I hadn't cleaned my room today! I was on my twelfth circuit when Mom tapped on my door. I came to a quick stop and waited for her apology.

She peeked in and said, "You have to stay in the house, not your room, you know." When I didn't reply she sighed and continued, "Anyway, I saw the box by your bedroom door. It was the modem, so I hooked up the Internet and tried it out for a while. Here's the username and password," she said handing me a piece of paper. I remained a statue, arms folded across my chest, so she dropped the paper on my dresser. "Well, I'm going to watch a movie in my room and then get some sleep. You can move about the house freely now without seeing me. Good night."

As soon as she closed the door, I fell back on my bed and

stared at the ceiling. Could this day get any worse? *Ring! Ring!* OK, maybe it could. It was Cade, and in the mood I was in right now, it wasn't going to be pretty. I barely got out a "hello."

"Is it true? Mouse told me you're on restriction. She didn't tell me why, but I'm assuming it's because of me. Well, is it?"

I unplugged the phone from my charger so I could lie back on my bed.

"Yes, I'm on restriction, practically for the rest of the summer. Mom has her mind made up, though, so the reason really doesn't matter." I could tell he was upset and pacing by the way his voice jiggled.

"It *does* matter, Ember. If you're in trouble because I was in your house, then it's wrong. You told me not to come in and I did anyway. I can talk to your mom and make her understand. I can get you off the hook."

It was a very appealing thought. I took a minute to think out. Number one: Cade wouldn't get in trouble for his escapade; well, maybe a slap on the wrist from his parents and the cold shoulder from my mom, but nothing like the punishment I was getting. Number two: It was the truth. He did come in when I told him not to, why shouldn't he be the one to pay? Thirdly, I really didn't want to spend the rest of my summer in this house, not when I was just meeting new people—something Mom even said I should do to prepare me for school.

"Ember, are you there?" Cade asked.

I told him to hold on while I continued to rack my brain for one reason I shouldn't let him be a scapegoat. I came up empty. "No?" I ventured timidly, shocked the word even came out of my mouth.

"No what? You didn't get in trouble because of me? Or no, you don't want me to talk to your mom?"

"No," I replied again with more confidence, "to both."

Suddenly, the truth was obivous. I did tell Cade not to come in, at first, but I did end up opening the door. It was a minor slipup, if you asked me, but he certainly didn't force his way into my house. There was another reason, a deeper motivation that I couldn't seem to uncover, but I had pondered it long enough.

"Look, don't worry about it. I'll be off soon and we can see each other again." Was that it? Was I protecting Cade or just making the most of a bad situation to protect myself from him? Why would I? Ugh, I was making my head hurt. I felt guilty just at the thought of it, so I added, "You were right about the box on the porch. Mom got the Internet hooked up so we can chat online, and I still have my phone..."

"Yeah, virtual you is definitely better than being together in person, Ember. That makes me feel so much better," he smarted.

"Hey, I'm the one stuck in this house for three weeks, Cade. You could try to make *me* feel better," I retorted. He was quiet for a minute then apologized.

"You're right, I'm sorry. It just doesn't seem like you care much about seeing me anymore. In fact, you said as much this morning, right before you slammed the door in my face."

"I didn't slam the door in your face. And if I was a little abrupt, it's because you were slinging weird accusations at me and wouldn't get out of my house!"

"OK, OK, I deserve that. Again, I apologize. I just haven't seen you for two days and I'm already dying. I don't know how I'm going to make it three more weeks," he moaned.

Then a thought struck me. "You *can* see me!" He was all ears then. "I do have permission to go to the teen group. You can see me there." He surprised me by agreeing.

"That's an awesome idea!" I felt happier immediately, and then he continued, "You can tell your mom you're going to church. Mouse can even pick you up and take you. Then, I'll meet you in the parking lot and we can take off for a few hours; we could hide out at our pond. Brilliant! How often does the church open its doors?"

"Cade," I said, as tolerantly as I could. "I didn't mean that I wanted to sneak off with you. I like the group, and besides, Mom already said she was the only one who could give me a ride. What I meant was, I want you to go to the meetings, too. We could see each other there." I didn't realize how much I wanted him to agree until it was out of my mouth.

"Oh, I see," he mumbled, obviously heartbroken. "Well, I guess I could think about maybe trying to make it sometime…"

"Really?" I asked hopefully.

"I said I would think about it, Ember. It probably doesn't even matter because, most likely, your mom is going to change her mind."

"Why?" I asked suspiciously.

"She was probably just upset about hearing gossip about you on her first day at a new job, that it made her look like a bad mother."

I had to admit; he made sense. Initially, I felt like she would calm down after a day or two myself, but I still wanted him to go to church with me.

"So, you'll think about church?" I asked.

Cade told me again that he would think about it, though his lack of excitement gave me doubts. I hung up the phone feeling worse than I had before it rang. Dejected, I went to my dresser and got out my pajama set. I moped across the hall to my bathroom for a shower and a ridiculously early bedtime.

When I awoke the next morning, the alarm clock displayed a disturbingly early time. I grabbed my cell phone to double check. It confirmed the sad truth; I was up at 7:00 during summer vacation. I threw my pillow over my head in frustration and tried to go back to sleep. Instead, memories of the nightmare hovered around my brain. I didn't want the day to end up like yesterday's fiasco, so I decided to start it out the right way. I sat on the floor by my bed and spent the next few minutes reading a few scriptures and praying. Then, I got ready for the day and prepared myself for the inevitable to-do list that I would find on the refrigerator. Surprisingly, there wasn't one. I guess Mom figured I had no life now, so I'd eventually get bored enough and turn into Martha Stewart. She could probably start contracting me out to the neighbors a couple of weeks into my sentence. *Ugh.* I had started to get ill again, something I was *not* going to be that day. I whispered a quick, silent prayer for what my grandmother called an "attitude adjustment," and grabbed a box of cereal, humming a song. Turns out, the whole praying thing was like riding a bike. I had done a lot of it when Mom first got married. I'm sure it kept me sane through those early weeks of transition. I couldn't remember why I had stopped.

I cleaned up the kitchen and my bathroom, washed a load of clothes, dusted the living room, and straightened my bedroom, all before lunch. I knew Missy would be working so I couldn't talk to her. I gave Cade a call, but he said he was right in the middle of something and would call me back later. A twinge of jealousy struck me, but I ignored it. I tapped my fingers on my nightstand, thinking. I really had to try to sleep in later tomorrow. I had no idea of what to do with the rest of the day. I had to be bored out of my brain to do what I did next; I called Mom to ask for advice. I could hear the roar of kids playing and crying in the background, so I knew she wouldn't be able to talk. She did manage to remind me the Internet was up so I thanked her (if her minute of shocked silence was a clue, she wasn't expecting that), grabbed the password off my dresser, and went in the office to find my computer.

The room was originally designed to be a bedroom. Mom had put a shelf on one side of the double closet for electronics and a tall filing cabinet on the other side. I found my notebook computer on the shelf. I sat down in the soft leather office chair and pushed Mom's computer aside. I set mine up and pulled up my account to check email and Facebook. I had dozens of comments on my wall and messages in my email. I had checked it while I was in Florida, but was too freaked out by everything that was going on to talk to anyone. The truth of that thought made me fall back into the chair with a sigh. I had only known Missy and Cade for a few days, but I felt closer to them and confided in them more than I ever did my so-called friends in Atlanta. I was spending more time praying and hanging out with Mom more often, too. Yesterday, I had been upset about being alone, but nothing could have been further from the truth.

I scrolled through my photo albums on Facebook with a detached curiosity. Who was that person? How could I have been so easily swayed into being just one of their clones? They didn't even like me in the beginning; I knew that for a fact. They made fun of my clothes and my ignorance of the latest music and movies. They laughed at my innocence. In retrospect, I believe they were jealous of it. By thirteen, most of these privileged girls had the money and freedom to do as they pleased. With little supervision, what brought them "happiness" was *anything but* sunshine and rainbows. I was just another meaningless diversion to them. Worse, I suspect my well-meaning, but clueless, stepfather asked them to take me under their wings, making me a charity case.

Armed with that knowledge, I sat up and deleted my Facebook account. I was about to do the same with my email account, but hesitated. My dad had set it up for me the last time I saw him a few years ago. I had only received a couple of emails since then, but decided I would keep the account and block everyone else but family. While I was deleting emails, I saw a familiar name, and was ecstatic I didn't miss it. Violet Denton had written me.

Violet was my neighbor and best friend during my elementary years. We promised to write each other every day when I moved, and managed to do so, for a little while. Eventually, the letters stopped, and then the phone calls became less frequent. We wrote by email when we got old enough for accounts, but they slowed, too, until finally, all dialogue between us stopped completely. I guess it wasn't unexpected for our long-distance friendship to fail. Although we were only a few miles apart, at thirteen, it might as well have been an ocean.

I leaned over the desk, chin in my hand, intent to feast on her every word; something that I didn't realize I was starved for until I discovered she had written. The subject line read *Re: Re: Re: Re: Re: Re: Hey, You!* I smiled. Violet must have discovered one of our old conversations. The latest was dated a week ago. She must have sent it right before I left Florida. I clicked on the email and was disappointed to find only a few sentences.

You probably don't remember me, but we were friends as kids. Anyway, I don't mean to bother you, but you've been on my mind a lot for some reason, so I thought I would just send you a quick note and say hi. I hope things are going well for you, Violet.

Disappointed, I read it again, thinking I must have missed something, some tenderness, the first time. "...probably don't remember me..." How could I not remember her? We practically lived at each other's apartments growing up. Our mothers purposely worked opposite shifts and "shared" us girls to keep down babysitting fees. Violet was like a sister to me, though we looked completely different. She was biracial; her mother had dark skin, while her father, based on the photo we used to hide and look at, had skin lighter than I did. Even at a young age, I realized Violet was a beautiful little girl. I had always been a little envious of her skin tone and curly dark hair. It reminded me of Missy's. I found myself grinning when I thought about our crazy, childish antics. It's amazing our mothers were still sane.

I started to write her back, but then I hesitated, unsure if I should keep the cool tone or not. I decided not.

What kind of crazy talk was that? Of course, I remember you, Curlee Q.T., and I want a complete update! Stat! And don't hold anything back...Sisters Forever, Green I'd Mbrr. I read over my response. She would get a kick out of my use of our old "handles," and the hospital lingo. We used to love to mimic our moms' jobs. Violet was so smart, I could easily see her as a doctor. Either way, we spent more time repairing our baby dolls' broken bodies than we spent feeding or rocking them. I touched the computer screen, willing Vie to write back soon.

I surfed the Internet for a while, looking at what was soon to be my new school, some music and movie sites, and the weather to see if there was going to be any relief from the heat anytime soon (no such luck). When I got bored of surfing, I refreshed my email to see if Violet had already responded. No luck there either, but there was a new message from Missy's church. I guess I had written down my email address on the visitor card I filled out. It was an invitation to a conference this Friday night at 6:00.

All juniors and seniors from the churches around town were invited. The meeting was called, "Celebrate our Similarities in Christ" and was to be held in the recreation room. According to the flyer, there would be music, food, and more team-building exercises to help us "build bridges across our faith." It sounded like a fun way to meet more people my age, but I knew Mom wouldn't agree, so I let it go and went in the kitchen to find some lunch.

After I had eaten and put away the clothes I had washed, I got a call from Missy. She was done at work and wanted to know if I would like her to stop by. I actually laughed at the insanity of her question and begged her to hurry. I knew it wasn't against Mom's rules, but decided to give her a call and ask anyway, just to be on the safe side. I must have called during a break, because she told me she would call me right back on her cell phone. I hoped the fact that she wanted to talk, instead of just giving me permission, wasn't a bad sign. I chewed on my nails and paced in the living room, waiting for her to call. This restriction stuff was getting to me; I was getting paranoid.

The couple of minutes I waited for the call seemed like an eternity. I clicked on the phone with impending dread.

"I only have a few minutes left of my break. I was going to talk to you about this when I got home, but since you went out of your way to call and check with me about Missy coming over…"

I heard someone talking to her in the background. I tapped my foot impatiently.

"What was I saying? Oh yeah, I have decided to reduce your three week restriction by half."

"What? Why? Not that I'm not happy, ecstatic about it, but…"

Mom interrupted, obviously in a hurry to get back to her desk on time. "I told you, Ember. You acted terribly at first, but your attitude has really improved. That and I might have overreacted a bit from the extra stress lately, you know? I'm sure nothing happened, but the rule about not having guys over when I'm not there still stands. And you're still on restriction through next Wednesday. Is that clear?"

"Uh, sure, yeah, of course," I muttered, confused but happy that she would reconsider.

We hung up and I did a little dance around the room. Tuesday was almost over, that meant…wait, did she say through next Wednesday? That meant I would taste sweet freedom next Thursday morning…only seven and a half days left to rot indoors! *I'm going to beg Missy to pick me up at 12:01 a.m. so we can go cruising! Hmm, I guess I should talk to Mom about curfews.*

My happy thoughts were interrupted by a knock at the front door. I snatched it open with a grin. "Hi!" I exclaimed.

She looked around nervously. "What's going on? Did I just see you dancing through the window?"

I grabbed her arm and pulled her into the living room. "You will never guess what happened!" I challenged and did a little bounce, unable to contain my excitement.

"Your mom let you off the hook?" she asked.

I deflated instantly. "Wha…? How did you know?" I asked incredulously.

"Well, first of all…," she said looking around the room. I realized this was the first time she had been in my house. "…what else could have made you so happy?" She had a point. "Also, Cade already told me about it."

"Cade already told you about it," I repeated. "Missy, I know we live in a small town full of gossips, but there is no way Cade could have known. I just hung up the phone with my mom.

Remember my dance?" I asked, shaking my hips a little as a reminder.

"Ember, why do you think your mom would let you off in less than twenty-four hours? Good behavior?"

"Well, yeah, that's what she told me," I muttered as I plopped down in the armchair.

"Well, Cade probably asked her not to let you know for some reason. I guess I shouldn't have even said anything," she said with a sigh.

I just sat there, brows creased, looking at my phone. Finally, I looked over at Missy, who had taken a seat on the sofa. "I told him last night not to tell Mom it was his fault. He didn't make me open the door. Why didn't he just let it go?"

Missy shook her head with a smile, "Wow, you're clueless sometimes."

"Most of the time," I corrected, "but what do you mean?"

Cade has been hanging around the restaurant constantly, absolutely miserable that he can't see you. Of course he talked to your mom. He would have brought over picket signs if he thought it would have helped. Can we talk about something else? I've said way too much already."

"You *have* said a lot," I said, astonished.

"Thanks," she responded cynically.

"No, it's a good thing. I like the talkative Missy."

"Ember, I told you before, I'm not really that shy; not when I get to know someone. I just end up sticking my foot in my mouth a lot. I mean, I was only in your house for a matter of seconds before I spilled the beans about Cade," she said, voice heavy with regret.

I knew I had to change the subject fast or she was going to "go clam" on me again. "I used to be good friends with someone with curly hair like yours," I said, thinking of Violet again.

"Two in one lifetime, huh; that's about the equivalent to lightening hitting twice in one spot, isn't it?" she quipped. "At least I'm not the only one with this frizz." I watched her pull at her hair self-consciously and the decision was made.

"If nothing else, my last four years equipped me with mad hair skills. Come on, let's see what we can do," I said, leading the way to my room.

We spent the rest of the afternoon in my room. By the time Mom walked in and surprised us, I had given Missy a full makeover, including hair, makeup and nails. She now had soft, glossy ringlets cascading down her back.

"You look beautiful!" Mom exclaimed with sincerity to Missy.

"Thank you," she replied shyly, once again reverting to the girl I first met. Mom asked her if she would like to stay for dinner, which sent Missy into a panic. "Oh no, I forgot; I promised I would take Karen's shift tonight!" she exclaimed, grabbing her things.

She didn't have to thank me for the makeover. Her hug and smile said it all. I quickly walked her to the door and waved bye as she hurried to her car.

Mom was in the kitchen, looking around in the fridge for leftovers. She pulled out some Tupperware and walked over to the pantry. "I thought you wanted to stay away from anything that had to do with the last four years in Atlanta, but seeing you two elbow-high in makeup and hair products certainly reminded me of that time. Are you OK?"

She was right, giggles over hair and makeup was something I equated with being "fake"; now I wasn't so sure. "I guess I was never into that stuff before you married Bill, so I just thought I liked it because they did; I just got into it so I would fit in."

"And now?" Mom asked and started opening cans.

"And now, I don't know what *I* like yet, but... that's it, I guess. I haven't figured it out, but I had fun today with Missy and it didn't matter if she was tall, pretty and rich or not. I think that's the difference isn't it? Just liking people for who they are, not because of what they do or don't have?"

Mom put down the food and wiped her hands on a dishtowel. She walked over, knelt down in front of me, and said, "I think you're wrong. I think you have absolutely figured it out and I'm so proud of you, honey." She reached up and gave me a big hug. We wiped away our tears and she went back to work on dinner. I washed my hands to set the table and remembered to tell her "thank you" for reducing my sentence. She told me "you're welcome" and went over to boil some noodles.

"Mom?" I asked tentatively. She looked up from the pot of water.

"Hmm?"

"Did Cade talk to you today about coming in the house yesterday?"

She leaned back on the counter and nodded.

"I told him not to," I said, afraid she might suspect I put him up to it.

"I know that, Ember. He told me everything; how you told him not to come in, then just to stay in the hall until you checked your phone." She sighed, walked over to the pantry and pulled out the noodles. "I was very angry with him, of course. He should have listened to you and stayed outside..."

"But, I..."

She held out her hand and continued, "But you didn't have to open the door. Like I said, I was very angry with him, but then I realized that you both were trying to protect each other. You could have told me it was his fault later that night when I calmed down, but you didn't. In fact, he asked me to not even tell you he called because you told him not to. Is that right? You told him not to 'fess up about his part in all this?"

I nodded, still holding our plates.

"Well, like I said, the fact that you both care enough to take the heat for each other is pretty special. That's why I couldn't stay angry with him very long. Cade made a mistake, Ember, but he obviously cares a lot about you and friends like that don't come along very often."

I was speechless for once. I didn't know how to take any of it so I just went back to setting the table.

"I still believe things were moving way too fast in the romance department, so in one way, I'm glad this happened, to put some space between you guys."

"Yeah. OK, Mom," I said distracted.

She added the noodles to the pot and turned around thoughtfully. "You know, just because you're on restriction doesn't necessarily mean you two can't see each other." That pulled me from the fog quickly.

"What do you mean?" I asked.

"The rule is, you can't go anywhere without me. Well, it turns out that Cade's Mom has invited us over for dinner tomorrow night. How would you like that?"

How *would* I like that? Mom had just agreed to let me see Cade again. I should be overjoyed and doing a dance like I did when she reduced my restriction time by a week and a half. Instead, I just felt…worried, happy, dread? What was wrong with me? She was right; Cade liked me a lot and I liked him, too. He was easy to talk to, fun to be around, and had shown he was a loyal friend; so why wasn't I whooping for joy and hugging Mom's neck right now? Based on the quizzical look she was giving me, she was probably asking herself the same thing. I had to drop the tough questions immediately and start acting like a girl who was happy to see her friend, or Mom would start asking the tough questions. The thought of that made me squirm, then jump into action.

"I think that's great, Mom! Awesome!" I said with a big smile, hoping it looked genuine. She went back to cooking, so I guess I passed. "Guess who sent me an email?" I began, steering the conversation down a safer road.

After the kitchen was cleaned, Mom went to relax in her room and I took a hot shower and retreated to mine. My hair was still dripping wet, and I was wrapped in a towel when Cade called. "Hi. So you talked to my mom, after all?" I asked, cutting to the chase.

He stuttered a minute in surprise, but finally admitted he did. "How did you find out about it? Did Missy rat me out?"

"Mom and I just had a long talk," I said, ignoring the question. "It seems that your act of bravery has inspired my mother to forgive you, reduce my prison sentence, and accept an invitation to a dinner party hosted by your mother in one fell swoop."

"You can make it up to me later," he said with a smile in his voice.

You impossible flirt, I thought.

"You could have really screwed things up worse, you know," I chided, determined not to let him off the hook that easily.

"But, I didn't," he argued. "Everything *is* better. Oh, sorry your mom didn't drop the whole restriction, by the way. I guess she had to keep her pride."

"You are exasperating!" I sighed and went over to my dresser and pulled out some pajamas.

"Yeah, that's why you love me," he flirted. "How about I drop by right now? Your mom's home, so it should be OK."

"No way," I snapped and immediately regretted being so short with him. "Sorry. Can you hold on a minute?" It was difficult to talk in a towel. I quickly got dressed and picked up the phone, towel drying my hair as I continued. "I just don't want to push it with Mom. I mean, she compromised a lot today, and like you said, she still has her pride." I finished and waited to see if he was appeased.

"Yeah, I guess you're right," he said after a long minute.

I let out a relieved sigh. I was really going to have to deal with my feelings soon; soon but not now.

"I guess a virtual you will have to do. You've got a webcam, right?"

We made a "date" on the computer for 9:00. I finished getting dressed, read a couple of verses in Mom's Bible, and stopped by to let her know Cade and I were going to chat. She seemed fine with it, as long as I kept the office door open. I set everything up, but he wasn't online yet, so I checked my email. I got a response back from Violet!

She wrote, *Wow, it's good to hear from you—I mean the "real" you. I've really missed you a lot Green I'd Mbrr! I'm doing great. I was granted a scholarship to a private school in California, near my extended family. I moved out here the summer before my freshman year. It's hard to believe we haven't spoken in two years!*

I spent the summer in GA and just got back to CA last week. I was helping Mom move to a small town outside of Atlanta to live with my Granny full time. I wrote to you a few days before I left, but I guess you didn't get it in time.

OK, I gave you some details—tag, you're it! Sisters Forever, Curlee QT.

I leaned back and ran my fingers through my hair. It was amazing to hear from Vie, but it was a lot to take in. Reading her "real me" comment and discovering she now lived on the other side of the country made my heart ache. Finding out I only missed seeing her by a few days sent me reeling. Is it possible to laugh and weep at the same time? It's strange; I had always assumed Violet would stay right here. I guess it's true, "you don't know what you've got until it's gone." I sat back up to write a reply when Cade rang in on a video call. I took a deep breath to get a grip on my emotions and answered the call.

I wasn't really in the mood to talk to anyone, but Cade and I ended up having a really good time. I had forgotten how easy it was to talk to him. He read to me from his favorite book and showed me his CD collection. I told him about Violet, how much I missed her, and about my day with Missy. We even made a three-way call to her so he could see her hair. He was very impressed. We all cut up and just enjoyed the rest of the time together. It made me look forward to getting through this weird transition phase, or whatever it was, and just being normal again. After two or so hours, we all said our goodbyes and signed off. That night, I took extra time to thank God for my friends. I never wanted to take them for granted again.

I woke up feeling refreshed the next morning. I think spending time with friends, in person and virtually, really set my mind at ease. I'd also had a long talk with God and did some interesting reading last night before I fell asleep. I began reading Jesus' words, the red verses, in the New Testament. Missy had advised that it was a good place to start; I had to agree. I flipped back open to where I left off, wanting to get in a few more verses before I started my day. Eventually, my back started aching a bit so I got up to stretch it out. I side stretched toward my bedside clock, which told me it was 10:00. I had been reading for over an hour! I laughed at the absurdity of it. Me, spending that much time reading scriptures, was unbelievable; of course, all of those little scriptures listed in the middle of the page took a long time to look up. I grabbed my phone, smiling and shaking my head on the way to the bathroom for a shower. I wanted to hurry and get ready. I had a big job planned for today.

That afternoon after I had eaten, straightened up, filled Violet in on the last three years of my life via email, made a dessert for dinner, and spent time on the phone with my grandmother, Missy, and Cade, I knew I had to stop avoiding the issue. The conversation with Cade a minute earlier had only strengthened my resolve. I silenced my phone, grabbed a pen and paper and sat on the middle of my bed. I took a deep breath and thought about him. The way I saw it, I had three choices: to be his friend, his girlfriend, or neither. I wrote all three on paper. The first decision was easy; I drew a line through "neither." I didn't even consider not having Cade around as an option. I knew I wanted to be his friend, too, so I circled it. *GIRLFRIEND* glared at me as I chewed my pen and considered it. Mom and I both felt it was moving too fast, and he had something against church, which made me wonder how it would work out when I wanted to go on teen retreats and such. Would he always be angry with me for it? When I thought about it honestly, I realized those two concerns made me uncomfortable around Cade. I knew I could talk to him about both, but he had already gone off on me about church; as far as moving too fast, the best way to slow down a relationship was to stay friends. I tapped the pen against the paper as I waited to build up the nerve, and then drew a line through *GIRLFRIEND*. I would tell him tonight.

By the time Mom got home from work, we only had an hour

until the Malones' dinner party. After a quick hello, she went to her room to get ready. I had already done my makeup and hair. I guess the time with Missy that week had inspired me to try something different so I used a curler to put loose spirals in it. I peered into my closet, trying to decide what to wear. I thought about the green silk dress, but after remembering Cade's reaction, I thought it might send a very different message than the one I wanted to convey. Finally, I chose a simple, knee length, aqua jersey dress with spaghetti straps. I added a strand of long, colorful beads, put on gold strappy flats, grabbed my phone and met Mom in the hall. She looked nice in her light slacks and airy, floral top. We complimented each other, grabbed my dessert and were on our way with five minutes to spare.

I had never been to Cade's house at night. The lightscaping up the walkway and around the flowerbeds gave it a more elegant feeling. Mrs. Malone and Cade were at the door to welcome us. I didn't see Mr. Malone. The moms chatted sociably as they took my Chocolate Delight to the kitchen. Cade closed the door behind me and smiled his trademark grin. It was a nice change from the last time I had seen him in person. I felt a little twinge of guilt when I thought about what I was going to tell him later that night, but I pushed it away. He started to tell me something but was interrupted by someone loudly clearing her throat behind him.

"So, do I get an introduction?" asked the bleached blonde behind Cade. He moved aside with a sigh. "Ember, this is Camille."

"You should have told her I'm your big sister, doofus," she corrected him with a playful slap to the back of his head. "And you are...what?" she inquired with an eyebrow raised in disdain.

"Back off, Cami," he warned, pulling me further into the living room.

I took a seat on the sofa and distractedly petted Snowball. I could hear our mothers putting the finishing touches on dinner. Cade volunteered to get me a drink, and then left me alone with his sister. She sat on the edge of the armchair with crossed legs. There was only the snapping sound that echoed through the room, as she repeatedly slapped her left flip-flop against her heel. I tried to sneak a quick peek at her, but her hair was mesmerizing. She had managed a "just got out of bed" look without it being a tangled mess, quite a feat for someone with waist length tresses. The old me would have eyed her roots, but I kept my eyes below her forehead. She wore a simple summer dress that must have come out of her old stored clothes; she looked like she would be more comfortable in black fishnets paired with combat boots.

"I really like your hair," I said finally to break the uncomfortable silence.

Cade handed me a glass of iced tea before his sister could respond. I'd only had time for a sip when Mrs. Malone called us to dinner. Cade held out his elbow and started to lead me in when a hand smacked the back of his head, surprising us both. He stopped and rolled his eyes, but dutifully held out his other arm, which Cami promptly grabbed. The three of us strolled in the dining room, but came to a screeching halt when Cami put on the brakes.

"What is *he* doing here?" I heard her whisper to Cade with venom in her voice.

Mrs. Malone must have noticed our little frozen group—it would have been difficult not to—because she immediately jumped up from the table to fix things. "Hey kids! You know

I have a great idea!" she proclaimed with false enthusiasm. "I doubt you want to sit around here and listen to our boring adult talk. Why don't y'all grab a plate and take it upstairs to the TV room?"

Cade must have thought it was a great idea, because he grabbed two place settings and turned to hand them to us, but Cami just stood there like a rock, arms folded across her chest. He just shrugged and took one himself, filling up his plate.

"It looks delicious, Mrs. Malone," I complimented, glancing at Mom to see if she felt as uneasy as I did. She had a tight smile glued on her face, so I finished quickly. I thought things would improve greatly once we got out of the way with Cami. On the way out, I impulsively grabbed an extra place setting and left as quickly as one can without being in a dead run.

Cami was already in a black recliner when Cade and I entered. I set the plates on the coffee table, divvied up the food, and handed one to her. She stopped clicking her flip-flop and looked at me in surprise. She didn't say anything, but took it. After a second, she started eating with gusto, so I guess that was a good sign. Obviously, being wolfishly hungry ran in the family, I concluded, watching the two of them. Before I got halfway through mine, Cade was done and left to get Cami a drink and seconds for him. I assured him I was fine; so I was, once again, left alone with Silent Big Sister.

"He's infatuated with you, you know," she said abruptly as soon as Cade shut the door behind him, making me drop my fork.

I looked up in surprise. "We're just friends," I explained.

"May...be," she said, laying her plate on the floor and turning to face me, "but not by his choice." She crossed her legs and began snapping her sandal again. I felt like a bug under a microscope.

"We haven't even known each other that long. I mean, he may have a little crush on me, but..."

"I've seen Cade have crushes; many, *many* crushes," she laughed, rolling her eyes, "but this; you are not one of them." I guess she saw the concern—or maybe guilt—in my eyes because she got serious and added, "Look, it's none of my business how you feel about him, but he's my little brother and he deserves to be happy. Something that's not easy to do in this place," she said with a wave of her hand.

I wondered what she meant. Cade always seemed to like his family a lot. She leaned closer to me and stared, making me squirm a little.

"I'm not here to look out for him anymore, and I can't make you do anything you don't want, but I'm asking you; please don't break my little brother's heart, OK?"

Just then, Cade burst in the door talking happily about snagging the last roll and saved me. Cami didn't take her eyes off me, though. She was waiting for my answer. I wanted to reassure her, to let her know that I cared for her brother, too. But with Cade there, I could only nod my head.

It must have been sufficient because she clapped her hands together once and belted out, "Who's ready for some Rock Band?"

The three of us played videos games on their giant screen TV until Cami's cell phone rang. The way her voice rose by a couple of octaves and went all bubbly, I assumed it was from a guy she liked, a lot. She unceremoniously dropped her bass in the nearest chair while chatting, nonstop. She paused when she got to the door, and held the phone against her stomach. "My chaperoning time is officially over. Babysitter, out." She gave us a curt salute and left the two of us, holding our drumsticks and guitar, staring at the door where she had just been.

"Well, that was abrupt," muttered Cade, taking off his guitar. "Wanna go outside for a little while?"

He shut down the game while I stacked up our dirty dishes to carry down. With his help, we brought them down to the kitchen and set them on the counter. We could hear our mothers chatting incessantly in the dining room. From the aroma, they had obviously just made coffee, which made sense. Only high doses of caffeine could make someone talk that fast. There was no sign of Mr. Malone, but I could see the light from under the door of the office, so I assumed he was hiding out in there.

Cade slid open the glass door for me and calmed Raven before she jumped up on me. I petted her and then looked around in awe at the back yard. There were lights everywhere; strings of lights on the deck, lanterns in the trees, and glowing, floating flowers in the pool. He watched me as I took it all in, and then took my hand and we walked to the pool. He opened the metal gate for me and we sat at a little white metal table with matching chairs. Cade picked up a lighter and lit the candle that sat between us.

"I'm sorry about dinner tonight—for the thing that happened between Cami and my dad. She can be really awful sometimes, especially when it comes to him." Cade wouldn't look me in the eyes, he just twisted the lighter through his fingers.

"It's OK, Cade. Your mom was right. We probably would have been bored out of our skulls sitting in there listening to them reminisce about our toddler years, and arguing about the best way to dress a window."

He looked up and seemed hopeful.

I continued, "Besides, your sister is…Cami seems like she is comfortable in her own skin and knows what she wants, ya know? I like that. I like her."

I hadn't really thought about it before, but now that I had said it, I knew it was true, even if she scared me to death. My comment did the trick. Cade's smile was back. Then, his mood turned pensive.

"It hasn't been the same around here since Cami left right after Christmas. She wasn't supposed leave until next month, but she had finished all of the credits needed to graduate high school early, so she moved out."

"She was just a senior this past year? You two must be close in age, then."

"Yeah, we're about eighteen months apart. We're close in age and just close, I guess. Sometimes she acts more like my mom than my sister, though," he said with a chuckle. "This is the first time she's been home since she left and that's only because she thought Dad was out of town this week. His trip got canceled, which caused the blowup at dinner."

I was going to ask Cade why she hated his father so much, but felt like I should let him talk about it when, and if, he was ready. Instead, I said, "It's really OK, about dinner. I've really enjoyed tonight. I had a lot of fun with your sister."

Cade stood up and reached out for my hand to help me to my feet. "Yeah, but I never got to tell you how beautiful you look."

We stood facing each other. His intense look made me suddenly feel shy. I looked down and pointed out, "You just did."

I felt his hand gently move my hair back from my face. I looked up as he slowly moved forward to kiss me, but I quickly took a step back.

"Cade, I...I mean, we..." I began.

I hadn't forgotten to tell him that I only wanted to be friends. It seemed like I had no choice but to tell him now, though I didn't know how to say it. The conversation I had with Cami earlier came flooding to my memory. I hadn't thought it was that big of a deal when I made my decision; now I felt extra pressure to make sure I didn't hurt him. I obviously needed more time to think about what to say.

"Never mind," I whispered, frustrated.

Cade must have taken my decision not to protest as a sign because he leaned forward and kissed me. It was a gentle, sweet kiss, one that confirmed what Cami had told me. I looked up into his eyes and found the same emotion.

"Ember!" We quickly broke apart, both shaken.

Mom continued calling from the back deck so we silently made our way toward her. Halfway through the yard, I paused and listened. For a second I thought I could hear a snapping sound, but decided it was my imagination. Cade and his mother escorted us through the house and waved from the front porch as we drove away.

Chapter Five

I SPENT THE NEXT day and a half throwing myself into work. I was tired of thinking. Cade had called a few times, but all of our conversations were superficial and short. I think he must have sensed my frustration and had made the decision to lie low until I was free to date again. By mid-morning Friday, I had officially unpacked our last box. I called Mom at work to share the good news. She obviously felt it was worth celebrating because she picked me up on her lunch break and we went to Missy's restaurant for lunch.

The familiar bell jingled on the door as Mom and I entered. The place was packed with the lunch crowd. Most of the patrons, like Mom, were only designated the 12:00 hour to eat and the cafeteria-style lunch was a great alternative to fast food. We slowly made our way through the crowd to the beginning of the line. I chose chicken and dumplings as my main dish, with butter beans, field peas, and pecan pie as my sides. Behind me, Mom must have approved of my selections, because when I looked back to her for money, her plate was loaded down with the same.

We sat down at the only empty table left, a four top with pink flowers on the tablecloth and one in the vase to match.

"I think the fresh flowers are such a nice touch," Mom

observed. "Oh, speaking of flowers, Rose…Mrs. Denton was able to find me through your conversations with Violet. It turns out, she and her mother live only about twenty miles from here. She asked if we would come over for a visit tomorrow. What do you think?"

I knew all of the boxes were unpacked, which left the way clear for more labor-intensive housework, so I thought a Saturday away from the house was a great idea. I told her it sounded great, so we agreed to leave the next morning after breakfast and focused on our lunch.

After we both had eaten our fill, we pushed back our plates and started on our pies. We were discussing how marvelous it was when Missy walked up in her work uniform: a bright yellow t-shirt that read *Johnson's Family Cookin' Cafeteria*, jeans and a white apron folded in half around her waist. She carried a small round tray with coffee, cream and sugar and gave Mom a timid smile. I raised my eyebrows at Mom and she took the hint.

"Oh, thank you, Missy. I would love some coffee." Mom poured herself some creamer and added, "I still can't get over how beautiful your hair looks. You girls did an amazing job. I might have to get you two to work on mine," she added, pushing it out of her eyes.

For someone who was accustomed to top of the line stylists for the last three years, my working on Mom's hair was an intimidating thought. Missy interrupted me as I was mentally styling hair when she sat in one of the extra chairs.

She cleared her throat and asked in a louder voice than necessary, "So, Ember, are you going to the teen conference at my church tonight? You know, the one that Pastor Eric sent you a personal invitation to?"

I gave her a questioning look. The "personal invitation" had been an email blast, and besides, she knew I couldn't go.

"I'm on restriction, remember Missy?" I responded.

"Oh, that's right. I forgot," she said, sounding like a bad actor reading lines.

I knew she was up to something but hoped Mom would just think she was strange.

"Well, you should tell Pastor Eric," she instructed.

"I guess you'll just have to give him my regrets, Missy. I don't have his number," I sighed.

"I have a better idea," she said as she jumped up from the table, making Mom's coffee cup teeter.

Mom steadied the cup and gave me a quizzical look. I just gave her a shrug and went back to my pie. A few minutes later, we were rising to leave when Pastor Eric walked up and asked if he could join us for a second. I could tell Mom was tempted to look at her watch to see if she would be late, but manners kept her from doing so. There was a clock on the wall behind her. I saw she had time so I answered for her.

"Sure, Mom still has twenty-five minutes left to get to work."

She gave me a quick look of relief then turned as I introduced the two of them.

He shook Mom's hand and spoke quickly, "I won't keep you two long. I just saw Missy and she mentioned that Ember wouldn't be able to make it tonight. Of course, I was really hoping she could. We could use someone who is new to the area to help give us a fresh perspective. The meeting is all about how teens can come together across denominational lines and support each other and our community. We're very excited about it." His eyes never left Mom, which made me wonder exactly who he was trying to convince.

I cleared my throat to get his attention. "I would love to come, Pastor Eric, but I'm on restriction." I gasped when I felt a soft kick in my shin, presumably from my mom, because she corrected me.

"I never said you couldn't go to church, honey. I'm sorry, Pastor. Ember and I must have just had a miscommunication. Of course, she'll be there."

"No harm done," he said with a chuckle. "I know all about the hazards of communicating with teens."

"By the way, please call me Eric."

"OK," Mom said, looking demure, "and I'm Kim."

Missy slipped into the fourth chair about that time. She leaned over and whispered in my ear. "He's single, you know."

The look of horror I shot her must have conveyed my meaning better than words, because she gave me an apologetic smile, and then bolted.

※

Mom dropped me off in front of the teen center a few minutes before seven. The confidence I felt, compared to the previous visit, was reassuring, although I was still nervous about meeting so many new people. I was more appropriately dressed this time, I hoped. I was wearing jeans and a smoky grey silk tank top; it was still a designer outfit, but at least it didn't require heels. I waved bye to Mom, thankful she didn't suggest coming in to see Pastor Eric. The idea was preposterous, but Missy had made me paranoid. When I looked back, Missy was there leaning against the open door, obviously anxious for me to come inside the building.

When I walked in, I understood her urgency. The room was almost full to capacity with teens, many of whom I didn't recognize. All of the chairs that had previously been pushed against the facing walls were now positioned in the center of the room toward the stage. A band was there, moving around microphones and tuning their instruments. The door to the café was propped open and the smell of pizza filled the room. There was a rope across the entrance to the video games, leaving it deserted. Most of the people were milling around in the seating area or were already seated and talking in small groups. Missy told me there were seven churches represented, putting the total at around two hundred and fifty. There were two girls sitting at a long table by the door whom I recognized from our group. One of them asked for my email address and phone number while the other crossed my name off a list. Then, I was handed a nametag and a plastic bag that resembled something I would get at the mall. While Missy continued to fill me in with details, I checked my bag of goodies and found a program of the night's events, a blue strip of cloth, a composition notebook and pen, a ticket—presumably for a drawing—various church flyers and a Christian teen magazine; nice. I pinned on my nametag as Missy led us to our seats in the front row; she had obviously gotten here very early.

After we took our seats, a few teens from our group came up and chatted with us. A few strangers, brave enough to leave the safety of their groups, also stopped by to introduce themselves. Noah, a tall guy with reddish-brown hair, seemed to have really hit it off with Missy. They were both shy, so their attraction to each other was hard to catch. I drew my conclusion based on the degree of her blush. I butted in and said I was surprised they didn't know each other, considering there were so few people around here. It turned out that Noah attended a small, private Christian school in town, was relatively new to the area, and had never had the pleasure of eating at her parent's cafeteria;

something he promised to remedy soon. The two of them were comparing their favorite bands when the microphone let out an earache-inducing screech, cutting their conversation short. Noah and everyone else standing around quickly took their seats as Pastor Eric apologized for the noise. After everyone was seated and relatively quiet, he extended a friendly welcome and enthusiastically introduced the band, who entertained us for the next hour.

Next, a representative from each group was asked to come on stage, where they introduced their teen group, telling a little about their accomplishments and goals for the upcoming school year. I was surprised that Noah spoke for his group and was also surprised when Missy let out a frustrated breath and slumped in her seat after he finished. I sent her a quizzical glance. The look I got in return let me know her reaction wasn't open for discussion. After Noah finished speaking, Lorie, a girl from our group, presented our introduction. She talked about the upcoming party we were planning, the ski trip over the winter, and beach trip in the spring. Our group's goal was "to have tons of fun in a safe environment." It was my turn to slump a little after the next presenter talked about her group's plans to feed the hungry, minister to the unsaved, and grow in Christ.

Missy just rolled her eyes and whispered, "Show-off."

After all of the representatives were through with their introductions, Pastor Eric thanked them and told us, by the end of the night, we would have at least one objective that our group would achieve together this year. Everyone clapped and he sent us to our next planned activity: team building. We were instructed to find our teams by tying the colored strip of cloth somewhere on us and trying to find others with the same color. I noticed some people were putting theirs on inconspicuously, but I decided to go for obvious and tied it around my arm. Missy pulled a red cloth out of her bag, and I felt disappointment wash over me as I realized we were on different teams. I guess it was to be expected since this was all about getting to know other people, but it didn't help me feel any better. She gave me a quick reassuring hug as we wished each other luck; then, we went on our color search.

An hour later, we had finished three games. Although I didn't like the color method, I had to admit it worked. I was one of the fifteen on the blue team and didn't know anyone, at first, but knew each of their names and a little about them by the time we were done. I noticed that by splitting the group up, the whole dynamic of the meeting had changed. Before, most everyone had stayed within their circle of friends; now there was much more talking outside each church group. Even though I liked the other teens, I still wanted to hang out with Missy. I had just grabbed a piece of pizza, chips, and lemonade from the concession stand when I spotted her through the window of the café. She was sitting at a two-top table with Noah, who I noticed had a red cloth wrapped around his wrist. Disappointed for me, but happy for her, I backed away and bumped into one of my teammates. I remembered his name was Reid Connors. The only other two things I knew about him was he had black hair, ice-blue eyes, and was the quarterback of my soon-to-be school's football team.

"Ember, right?" he asked me. It was getting crowded and loud in the hall so I just nodded, balancing my food and drink. "Here, let me take that for you," he offered. He only had a drink, so I let him take mine and led him through the crowd, back into the teen center.

"Thanks," I said, taking my lemonade. "I guess there's nowhere to sit in there, so I'll just go back to my seat." I took a few steps to the stage when I noticed he was walking beside me.

"Do you mind if I join you out here? I hate crowds," he admitted.

His confession surprised me. I could definitely picture him at post-game parties surrounded by cheerleaders, but then I mentally scolded myself for stereotyping. I felt a little nervous at the idea of sitting alone with him. In my former life, we collected jocks like some girls collect bracelet charms. I sighed and assured myself that I was different now. *Talking to someone who happened to play football wasn't going to send me into a downward spiral, nor would it be betraying Cade,* I thought with a twinge of guilt. The meeting was set up to help build bridges, right?

"Of course," I responded. "I would like that."

The next few minutes passed surprisingly quickly. I found out more things about Reid and a lot more about my new school, like the best teachers and what foods to avoid in the cafeteria at all costs. Our conversation wasn't awkward at all and I was even able to meet a lot more people, as they took Reid's lead and came up to talk to me. By the time Missy returned, there were a dozen of us all talking and laughing. It felt good to just hang out with a group people and not be concerned about their social status. I was about to question Missy about Noah when Pastor Eric and his microphone, once again, painfully interrupted and sent everyone scurrying to their seats.

According to Pastor Eric, it was now time to decide on our collaborative goal for the year. We were instructed to take our belongings and find our teammates again, this time without the colored cloth. Once we were in our respective teams, we were to organize chairs into a small circle and use our notebooks to brainstorm until each group agreed on one goal and one alternate. He told us that the band would play one song while we found our team. We all had to be seated in our circle by the time they finished. Those who didn't make it in time would have to perform a song at the end of the night. As soon as the band struck the first note, there was chaos.

Everyone made it to his or her seat in time, but I think the band might have played a part in our success; there seemed to be a highly suspect number of repetitions of the chorus. Our team came up with the ideas rather quickly. One person proposed we collect shoebox gifts for the Samaritan's Purse Christmas drive. Someone else said we go a step further and volunteer to pack the boxes for shipping at the warehouse in Atlanta. I suggested a community Thanksgiving Dinner for the underprivileged as our alternate. I didn't say so, but my mother and I had benefited from a few of those when I was little, before she got her nursing degree. We all agreed on the choices and were the first group to finish. While we waited on the others, a few of the teens started talking about an evangelist who was going to be at one of their churches on Wednesday. They talked about things like healings and prophecy, which rather freaked some of us out. No one said anything to them; this meeting was supposed to highlight our similarities, after all, but I could tell the ones who were uncomfortable by their squirming. I probably should have been uncomfortable, too; I had never seen any healings or miracles. I guess I was just naïve because the prospect of people being healed of cancer or the blind seeing excited me, and I was fascinated by the thought of someone knowing the future. I said as much to them, to the surprise of a few from our group. Ella, a blonde girl who looked about my age, excitedly invited me and gave me directions to the service. Dimples punctuated her smiling face when I told her I would think about it.

We didn't get to talk about it anymore, but it was announced that everyone was finished. We stayed with our teams while a representative placed our number one suggestion in a box on the stage. Pastor Eric and the other teen pastors looked through them to find repeats. Out of the fourteen teams, six chose to cook for those in need, either at a church or to volunteer at a soup kitchen. The next most popular suggestion was to volunteer packing shoeboxes for Samaritan's Purse. After a quick break to confer, the pastors decided that based on our numbers, we should be able to do both. We would all host a dinner in November for Thanksgiving and volunteer at the warehouse in December. A few volunteers passed out a clipboard to each group so we could sign up to be on a committee to plan one of the events. I signed up to help organize the Thanksgiving dinner.

Pastor Eric returned to the microphone. He thanked the band and then us for our participation, saying he was looking forward to what this new alliance would do for our community. All of the other teen pastors then said a few words of closing. Next, Pastor Eric asked us to help by moving our chairs back in the rows against the two walls before closing prayer. I picked up my things and started to move the chair when Reid, once again, asked if he could help. I thanked him, but told him I had it that time.

He put a hand on my arm to hold me back while the others moved ahead. When they were out of earshot, he whispered loudly in my ear so I could hear over the noisy crowd, "Don't go to that meeting on Wednesday, Ember. Those people do crazy things, like play with snakes."

Until Reid mentioned it, I had forgotten I would still be on restriction. I hadn't really seriously considered going anyway so

I told him I wouldn't. He seemed relieved that I heeded his warning, so he walked away to help move chairs.

Once everyone had settled back down, Kyle, one of the guys from our group who went to church with Noah, stepped on stage to pray. He was cute with dark hair, skin, and eyes and was a couple years younger than me.

He took the mike and asked, "Can we all join hands in a circle?"

A lot of the kids, including me, looked around nervously but moved forward to the center of the room to hold hands.

He began: "Dear Lord, we are joining hands tonight to sig-nify our unity and love for each other and especially, our love for You. We, first of all, thank You for what You did on the cross..."

Each word that guy spoke went straight to my heart and exploded inside my chest. I don't think I had ever heard anyone pray like that. It was different somehow. I peeked around to see if the prayer had that effect on anyone else, but they all seemed to have their eyes closed, just standing there or praying quietly. I closed my eyes again and tried to figure it out. It wasn't his voice. I could hear him fine, but he wasn't yelling. The prayer wasn't that impressive, either. It was brave of him to pray in front of us and all that, but he obviously hadn't rehearsed. Finally, I gave up and tried to ignore the heat that warmed me, from inside out.

Mom knocked on my bedroom door the next morning to remind me about the trip we had planned. I woke up and found myself lying across the bed, fully clothed, with Mom's Bible open beside me. I had texted her around ten last night and she agreed, once I told her Cade wasn't there, to let Missy take me home. I hadn't made it in until well after midnight because the assigned bonding exercises at the conference worked *too* well; nobody had wanted to leave their newfound friends. I should have gone straight to bed when I got home, but my head was swimming with thoughts of healings and such, so I stayed up to research it more in the Bible. It was neat stuff, but I was paying for it that morning. I dragged myself off the bed to stretch my aching muscles and take a look at the damage. Both the ache and the damage were worse than I could have ever imagined. I groaned and laid my head over on my dresser. I probably would have fallen asleep there except I knew Mom would accredit our missing our visit to Mrs. Denton's to my staying out so late and promptly cut out all late night excursions for the next year of my life. With the threat of nine p.m. curfews hanging over my head, I slowly shuffled my way to the bathroom.

After a shower and the impromptu twenty-minute nap I took while attempting to put on my shoes, I felt much better. I texted with Cade and chatted with Mom on the way, so conversation and a good GPS, made the trip go by quickly. We pulled up by the curb of an adorable little white house with a picket fence, tin roof and pale rose-colored shutters. Flowering vines ran up the posts of the front porch, reminding me of a fairy tale cottage. We had only made it up through the front gate when Mrs. Denton came bounding down the steps. I was in front of Mom so I got the full impact of her enthusiastic bear hug. She even bounced a little as she held me. Finally, she pulled back but kept my face firmly between the flattened palms of her hands.

"Child, you have grown!" she exclaimed in surprise, as if she had expected me to remain the twelve-year-old girl she knew in the past. "You and Violet both grew like weeds. If your momma and I had any sense we would have put bricks on your heads!"

She laughed heartily and turned her attention to Mom. Mrs.

Denton's face grew solemn as she pulled Mom close and spoke words of sympathy to her. I assumed it wasn't for my ears, so I went on ahead to the front porch and took a seat on the swing. It was still early so it was hot, but not yet unbearable in the shade. Soon after, the two of them walked up. Mrs. Denton's arm was still around Mom's shoulder and she nodded her head as she listened intently. So intently that neither of them noticed I was there. I jumped up and grabbed the screen door before it closed behind them.

The inside of the house was as cute as the outside. It was a "shotgun" house, named so because you could shoot a gun in the front door and it would go straight out the back without hitting a wall. The front room was a quaint sitting room with hardwood floors and pale yellow walls, adding to the sunny feel of the room. Two identical rocking chairs sat facing the door with a small table and Tiffany style lamp between them. On either side of the rockers, there were two high backed chairs opposite each other. There were photos and white doilies covering every available surface and an upright piano against the wall behind the door. Just beyond the sitting room was a little dining area. Just beyond the small, round table was the kitchen. I could hear the teakettle whistling and could smell fresh baked cinnamon rolls. I had grabbed a quick bowl of cereal before we left home, but the smell of that bread made my stomach growl angrily anyway.

"Would someone pick up that kettle and stop it from whistling?" someone demanded from a room in the back of the house.

The interruption brought Mom and her friend out of their bubble.

"Of course, Granny," Mrs. Denton replied to the voice. "Kim and Ember are here, remember them? Are you going to come out of your room to visit with us?" She motioned for us to have a seat and went to get the tea.

A few minutes later she came back with someone I could only presume was Granny. She was a little old woman who didn't look a day younger than two hundred. Her head barely reached Mrs. Denton's upper arm and she was about the same size around as that arm, too. Mrs. Denton gently helped the ancient woman into a rocking chair beside me, wrapped her legs up in a blanket and told us she would be right back with some refreshments.

Mom chatted with Granny a little while, asking her about Violet and the rest of the family. It didn't take long to realize that while Granny looked feeble, her mind was as sharp as a tack. She talked about each of her kin in great detail. I found out that she wasn't Mrs. Denton's mother, but her grandmother, and she would be 104 years old in November! We also discovered that there were quite a few girl relatives in the family with flower names. Granny's name was Daisy Edwards, but she instructed us to call her Granny. By the time we had finished our tea and rolls, my eyes were drooping from lack of sleep. Mom and Mrs. Denton quietly took our teacups and plates to the kitchen for more conversation while Granny and I were lulled asleep by the roar of the air conditioner in the window.

I awoke with an eerie feeling that someone was watching me. Disoriented, I sat up and looked around in a panic. A crocheted throw fell from my lap to the floor as I moved to the edge of the seat. Then, I realized I was still at Mrs. Denton's house. I picked up the throw and looked around for my mom. Instead, I saw Granny wide-awake in the rocking chair, staring intently at me. I made a comment about sleeping too long and asked if she knew where my mother had gone. It turned out, Granny needed a refill on a prescription so Mom had gone with Mrs. Denton and would be right back with the medicine and some lunch for us.

After it was established that I was awake and we were alone, Granny began rocking; her eyes never left mine as she asked, "You have some questions for me, don't you?"

I had just asked her where my mom was. Other than that, I was blank. I was still trying to come up with an answer to the strange question when she began firing questions at me.

"Do you know my Jesus?"

"Yes ma'am."

"Do you read His Word?"

"Yes ma'am."

"Don't look at me like that," she ordered, seeing my look of concern. "I don't have enough time on the earth to waste words. We need to get to the meat of the matter. Now, do you talk to Him?"

"I...I do now, there were a few years that..."

"In what language," she interrupted.

"Excuse me?"

"In. What. Language?"

"Um, I took a year of Spanish but..."

"You're hungry, though."

"I just ate, but thank you anyway."

Maybe her mind wasn't as sharp as I thought. Granny stopped rocking and with a shake of her head argued quietly to the ceiling. I had the strange suspicion that she was complaining to God about me.

Finally, with a sigh she turned back to me. "You have ears to hear, girl; so hear me. You know the Lord, but know there's more than just that. There's more available to us and you know it. Just ask Him, baby girl, and keep on asking. Gifts of signs and wonders and miracles will come, just get to know Him first; that's most important, hear me?"

"Yes ma'am."

"You get to know Him, then ask Him and keep on asking, knocking on that door. He'll open it and you'll receive what you're looking for."

I decided not to bother asking for what; that was getting me nowhere.

"Have you seen any miracles?" I asked, almost afraid of the answer.

"Yes, child. When I was only a child myself, a few years younger than you, my parents took me to Azusa Street." She paused, lost in memories.

I didn't want to interrupt, but I didn't know how much longer we had until Mom and Mrs. Denton would return. I really wanted to hear this part.

"What was on the street?" I gently prodded.

"It was a revival, not just a street. The Lord moved in powerful ways during those years. I was young, but I'll never forget it. You and your generation...you will too, honey. You will see miracles."

"How do you know?" I wondered how she could be so certain.

"First, because, like I said, you're hungry. You're tired of just walking around this earth taking up space and looking pretty. You were called to do more...to *be* more. These are dark times; the darkest I've ever seen. And when there is great darkness, that is when the Light can be seen best." She must have read my puzzled expression because she sighed with a shake of her head. Then she continued, "I know because sometimes the Lord shows me things. He'll show you, too. Just ask. Take my hand, honey," she instructed suddenly.

I reached across the space between our chairs and carefully took her hand. At first, her small hand lay limply in mine and

I was struck by the frailty of it. Then, she squeezed mine with an unbelievable fierceness. I waited for a long couple of minutes in silence.

I was expecting a long, eloquent prayer from such an old saint, but she only whispered, "Fill her hunger, Lord."

I felt the familiar trembling in my heart. Warmth spread down my back and tears sprang to my eyes. With conviction I didn't realize I had in me, I whispered in agreement, "Yes, what she said. Please."

The next evening, I was sitting in the café at church thinking back to the strange morning the day before. Mom and Mrs. Denton had come in immediately after my heartfelt prayer. We went home soon after. I felt a little silly about the whole prayer thing and hadn't breathed a word to anyone about it. Suddenly, I was brought back to the present by Missy's hand waving in front of my face.

"Earth to Ember," she joked.

"Sorry," I replied, shaking the memory from my head. "I guess I was a little distracted."

"Congratulations, you have just won the understatement of the year award," was her sarcastic reply as she handed me the saltshaker like it was a trophy.

"So what's so important that you can't help plan the big back to school party? I mean we're talkin' the playlist, here," she said, shaking a paper at me. "It doesn't get much more important than this."

Thankfully, Pastor Eric walked in about that time and dismissed us with a closing prayer.

"Actually, I think I need to talk to Pastor Eric."

Missy flashed me a concerned look but in the usual Missy fashion, didn't pry. Instead, she just said, "Whoa, sounds serious.

I'll just go turn in this list. I'll meet you by the video games when you're ready."

I said thanks and walked over to wait my turn to talk to the pastor.

"Hi, Ember," he said when the crowd had thinned out, "I'm glad you came over. I've wanted to check on you. How have things been going since last Sunday night?"

I knew he was talking about my rededication, so I told him how I was reading the Bible and praying a lot. I admitted just how surprised I was that I enjoyed it. I thought it sounded terrible after I said it, so I apologized. He just laughed and told me that a lot of people were surprised that the Bible was actually a good read. I was nervous about talking to him about everything, but other than a couple of teens slowly making their way out and a few people cleaning up, the room was empty. I might not get another chance. I told him I did have a question about church if he had time. He nodded and gestured for me to follow.

We walked to his office by the stage. I sat on a bright red loveseat against the wall while he took a seat behind his small desk.

"Mrs. Cathy, would you hang around for a few minutes?" he asked one of the women who was helping straighten up.

I guess it was policy for us not to be alone. I hadn't thought about it, but it seemed like a smart thing to do. Mrs. Cathy said she would be happy to and busied herself across the room with some kind of paperwork.

Pastor Eric turned his attention back to me. "Shoot."

Suddenly, I realized I had no clue of what to say about Granny, so I started with a safer subject. "Some kids at the conference Friday night invited me to a revival at their church. It sounded really....um, interesting, but another guy told me I shouldn't go."

"Why would someone tell you such a thing?" he asked, exasperated.

"He said," I looked over to make sure no one could hear and continued, "he said they would have snakes."

Pastor Eric leaned back with a loud sigh and ran his hands through his hair, "I see." He leaned up and looked like he was trying to find the right words. "Ember, you said it sounded interesting, so I take it you would like to attend this meeting."

I nodded, so he continued.

"I believe that the Holy Spirit gives us gifts..."

"You believe in the gifts?" I interrupted, surprised.

He looked at me as if I had said something strange, but continued, "Of course, maybe not to the extent some believe, but...my point is, the Holy Spirit gives us discernment. That means if we walk into something that's not right—not of Him— then we'll know," he pointed to his chest, "in here. Now, when you first visited here you probably felt a little out of place or nervous, but that's not what I'm talking about. That's normal. You understand?"

"Yes, sir."

"Good, and don't call me sir," he reprimanded with a smile. "OK, number one: discernment. The Holy Spirit is our guide and He will guide you if you let Him. Number two: I know all of the pastors in this area and I know for a fact that none of them would have snakes in their church. A couple of them eat them, but that's another, very gross story."

We both smiled, but then he got serious again.

"Ember, I hate to say it, but there are people, good, church people who say hateful things about other church people because...well, most of it is just ignorance. That's why I initiated having the teen conference Friday night. I really wanted you guys to hang out with each other and, like the flyer said, appreciate your similarities. Christians may never worship the same way here on Earth, but we believe in the same God and, to me, that's most important. If you want to worship with other Christians, I certainly won't advise you against it, though if it's a revival they will probably have an evangelist who I don't know. I would just suggest you go there with someone you trust, an adult, to take you home if you start to feel too uncomfortable, OK?"

I nodded again and asked, "Do you think maybe you could get some of the youth group together for the trip and maybe go with us?"

Once again, he sighed and leaned back, "Truthfully, no, I can't. Not everyone in this area feels the way I do. I even took a risk to get the teen conference going and had to fight hard for it. In fact, one church bent under the pressure and bowed out at the last minute."

"You mean the ones who were going to host it?" I asked.

"Yeah. Unfortunately, there's no way I could get agreement from the board for that kind of teen trip. I'm sorry, Ember."

The truth about all of the ignorance and fear made me have a sick feeling in my stomach, but I was happy that at least Pastor Eric wasn't one of them.

"It's OK. Thank you so much for talking to me." I got up to leave, but then I decided to ask a little more. "Pastor Eric, do you believe in miracles and stuff?"

"You mean in the Bible? Yes, of course."

"No, I mean today."

"What I believe, and the belief of this church, is called Cessationism."

Mrs. Cathy interrupted politely and told Pastor Eric that she believed everyone was ready to go.

"Thank you, I'd better lock up." I walked to the door with him and Mrs. Cathy. "I'm sorry I don't have more time to discuss it now. We'll talk more next Sunday, but in a nutshell, it means that the miracles, prophecies and such in the Bible existed to help grow the church. They don't exist now because we don't need them anymore."

I spent many hours tossing in my bed that night with conversations replaying in my head. I heard Pastor Eric telling me there were no miracles anymore. I also heard Granny telling me she had seen them...and so would I.

The next three days went by in a whirlwind of study. The few times I talked to Cade were difficult. He was getting more and more irritated at not being able to see me. Most of our conversations ended in an argument. I didn't allow myself the time to worry about it too much. Instead, I threw myself into the study of the gifts of the Spirit, looking up Cessationism, as well as the opposing belief, Continuationism. I devoured the Bible for every scripture about it and even had Mom take me to the library for books with historical accounts, including a book on the Azusa Street Revival. By Wednesday, I was pretty well educated on the subject, but was no closer to having a logical answer.

By the time the night of the revival rolled around, I realized I wasn't looking for something I needed to believe with my head. It was just like the day I gave my life to Christ, when I had felt the tug at my heart. Just like salvation, I had to step out on faith. I closed and put away all of the books I had been studying and fell to my knees in the middle of my bedroom. I prayed for faith, strength, and discernment; but most of all, I prayed for an answer—not to my questions, but to this hunger for the truth. When I finished my prayer, I knew the revival was where I would find some of the answers. I knew I had to get there and I knew, without a shadow of a doubt, my life would never be the same again.

Chapter Six

THE TAXI DROPPED me off and I found myself, once again, standing at the curb of a church frightened and wondering how to make an escape. I took a few steps forward to the bottom of the steps. The lights from the double glass doors shone down on me. I could see the people wearing nametags inside. They were handing out bulletins and welcoming those inside the foyer. Still, I waited in the darkness. Two strangers lost in conversation came up behind me. One bumped into me, bringing me out of my fear-induced trance. He apologized and continued into the church. I felt that maybe there was safety in numbers, so I quickly stepped up behind the couple and followed closely behind through the doors.

A petite, brunette woman named Carol immediately walked up to me and asked me if this was the first time I had visited. I was relieved to have someone to talk to, in spite of the difference in our ages. I told her it was my first visit, which seemed to have made her day. She enthusiastically began telling me how excited she was that I was there and began giving directions that would make a flight attendant proud. The more my personal greeter kept speaking, the louder she seemed to become. Suddenly, I felt like I was in a spotlight. My fight-or-flight response kicked in and when she pointed to the direction of the bathroom, I almost made a run for it. Instead, I forced myself to keep my eyes on her nametag. C-A-R-O-L anchored me to the spot and the moment passed. She started talking about their teen programs. My eyes broke free and darted around the foyer at the other people chatting around me.

What if someone recognizes me? What am I doing here?

I tried to moisten my lips, but my mouth was dry. I looked back up at Carol and realized she had finished her speech and was looking at me curiously. I mumbled my thanks, turned around to make my getaway, and ran into some people who had just walked into the church. I made a small squeak of frustration and tried to squeeze my way between them. Their arms came up in a red rover move, surprising me.

"Ember?" one asked.

I looked up and saw Noah with Ella and Kyle, the two who had invited me. Noah looked surprised, but happy to see me there and asked how I knew about it. Kyle filled him in while Ella turned her attention to me.

"Hi," I said weakly.

"Are you lost?" she asked, putting an arm around my shoulder. "The service is this way."

"Oh yeah, I must have gotten turned around," I chuckled without humor and followed them into the auditorium.

I had been attending the services in the teen center but hadn't been in a normal service in a few years, but everything looked about the same. As the two of them scanned the church for seats, I looked around. Two double wooden doors led from the foyer. The part of the ceiling above us was low, so there must have been a balcony. Just ahead, there were three large sections of pews with two aisles leading to the front of the church. There was no wooden altar as I remembered, but stairs with medium green carpet wrapped around the half-circle platform. There were chairs in three tiers for the choir. Just behind them was a curtain, which I assumed covered the baptismal. I smiled at the thought of the pool back there. It was the last memory I had of being in church.

The two of them waved toward a group of teens about midway up the left section and motioned for me to follow. They introduced me to everyone, some I remembered from the conference. After the introductions were made, I stayed in my seat and just enjoyed listening to their chatter. I could see people milling around on stage, setting up instruments and giving last minute directions. I noticed the feeling of panic had subsided and a feeling of excitement took its place. Suddenly, I couldn't wait for the service to begin. I looked around at the people in the church to see if I was the only one. They were smiling and laughing quietly, but underneath the air was crackling with a sense of anticipation, like a famous band was about to walk out on stage. I felt the strange desire to grab my neighbor's hands and do a bunny hop squeal—something I hadn't done since Violet got a "do you like me check the box" note from the cute boy in our fifth grade class.

I noticed I was, literally, sitting on the edge of my seat. I scooted back and gripped my hands together, but allowed my leg to bounce with abandon. I looked over and grinned at the girl next to me. She grinned back and leaned over to tell me something but was interrupted by the drums that hit the opening beat. The rest of the band joined in, and a guy in a suit, who I assumed was the pastor, told everyone to stand. I actually felt relieved as I jumped out of my seat and started clapping as the choir made their way in singing and swaying to the music. The words were on the overhead screen so I sang along to a lot of the songs.

When the music slowed, the choir leader asked everyone to raise their hands and sing. I immediately felt self-conscious until he added, "those who have ears to hear, listen." It made no sense, but remembering the words Granny spoke to me that day, I did. I closed my eyes, raised my hands, and listened. As the song played, I kept waiting to hear some revelation, but instead I only felt something like a spitball hit me. I threw my eyes open and looked around but didn't see anything, so I went back to my meditation. Once again, something small and soft hit my hand. It was embarrassing. I could imagine some kids in the balcony, probably ones who knew I wasn't supposed to be here, throwing paper at me. I could just see my hair littered with giant white flakes. I couldn't look around again though; it would only fuel their fun; so I stayed in the same posture. Then, I felt more pelting but it didn't feel like paper. It felt like—rain? I felt tiny drops of water hitting my hands, but they weren't wet. I had to open my eyes again to see if anyone else felt it, but everyone seemed to be singing or praying quietly. I closed my eyes again and smiled at my own private rain shower. By the time the song ended and we were asked to be seated, the invisible water had made it up to my ankles. I grudgingly sat down and kept feeling my pants legs for wetness. My neighbor shot me a questioning look but I took the safest route and just shrugged.

After being introduced, the evangelist walked up and gently placed a worn, black Bible on the pulpit. He grabbed each side of it and stood there, head bowed. I guess I was expecting an old preacher because the blond-haired man around my mother's age took me by surprise. His long silence wasn't expected, either. There was no music or talking while he stood there praying. Instead, others around the congregation started bowing their heads and praying while some knelt in their pews with their heads against the seats. I just stood there, not sure what to do. Around me, the quiet prayers increased to a hum. The teens in my row all stood with their heads bowed, holding hands. The girl beside me reached over and I gave her mine. I had prayed a lot in my bedroom lately, but then, I couldn't think of a thing to say to God so I just kept my head bowed and waited. As I stood there, the air felt thicker—almost like I was standing outside on a foggy day. Once again, I was in awe and a little bewildered about the freak indoor weather changes, but I didn't want to move. I didn't want it to stop. Finally, the evangelist straightened himself up. He looked over the crowd; it seemed he made eye contact with each person there before he spoke.

"I had a message to preach tonight about faith, but God had other plans. He wants you to know that He loves you. Your Father loves you. He sent His only Son that whoever—it doesn't matter what you're wearing, who your daddy is, what you've done, who you are—*whoever* believes in Jesus will be saved."

The evangelist made the altar call and immediately people started moving out of their seats. I watched a middle-aged man weep into his mother's shoulder as she helped him up the aisle, tears streaming down her face. Young couples walked forward together, hand in hand. Men and women, young and old, people dressed in designer clothes and some dressed in rags, people with piercings and tattoos, businessmen and women, all quickly made their way to the front of the church. I thought about my own rededication at the teen group and understood their hurry. I found myself smiling once again and this time the water I felt running down my cheeks was visible to all, but I didn't care. I can't remember ever feeling this much joy when I saw these people giving their lives to Christ. Mrs. Dawson used to say the angels threw a party when a person was saved. I say it would be hard to imagine it being better than that very moment, fog and all.

People with nametags were making their way through the crowd praying with people for a while. Some were getting up and going back to their seats, faces shining. I thought the service would be over a lot sooner than I had anticipated. The thought of sneaking back in the house saddened me. The evangelist brought me out of my worried thoughts by asking a question that resounded within me.

He asked, "Is there anyone in this room who feels like there is more to this life? Who feels like God is calling them to do more than just to exist in this world?"

I didn't catch everything he said, because just those few words rang through me like a shout. I sat there, looking like a deer in headlights with my pulse racing in my ears and my palms sweating. Granny and I had both prayed for more but I didn't know it was going to lead to me having to make a fool of myself by walking up in front of all of these people. I decided to play it safe and stay in my seat. I sat there and moved my legs aside as the teens in my row went forward. I watched as most of the remainder of the church moved to the front. They all stood side to side until the entire front of the church was packed to capacity. I let out a breath of relief, knowing I couldn't fit anyway, but I still wanted to go. What if this was the chance to stop that feeling inside me . . . the one that told me there was something else I was supposed to do with my life? Without thinking anymore, I dashed out of my seat and went forward. There was no room to stand so I knelt there in the aisle, just behind the people. I guess I should have been worried about being stepped on, but I wasn't. I just wanted answers, but didn't know what to ask for. I remembered what Granny prayed that day. *Fill my hunger, Lord,* I whispered. One of the teens saw me and reached down. I took his hand and four or five others gathered around in the aisle. We all stood there in a circle. Kyle asked me what I wanted and said they would help me pray.

I felt tears running down my face and felt stupid, but said, not looking up, "I don't know."

He tenderly lifted my chin and smiled at me. Ella pressed a tissue in my hand. I smiled at her, wiped my face and waited for Kyle to talk.

"Ember," he said, "when you don't know what to pray the Holy Spirit can give you the words. Pray with us, but don't worry about what you say."

He smiled at me again then nodded at our little prayer group. They all bowed their heads and prayed quietly. I started praying in my head. After I said the equivalent to the Lord's Prayer, I listened and started making out some weird sounds. I realized I wasn't praying in English.

Kyle must have noticed I was freaking out because he leaned over and whispered to me, "Quit thinking, Ember, just pray out loud. Don't think about it with your head, you're more than that. Don't be afraid. We're here for you and we're praying for you."

I was overwhelmed by his gentleness and the thought of them praying for me. I nodded and bowed my head again and began praying. I wasn't loud but I did pray aloud with them. I quit worrying about what to say and just prayed. I felt the humming inside me again and electricity passing around our little circle. All of our voices melded together for a while, and then I noticed I was praying alone. I stopped and looked around at five grinning faces. A cry of joy racked my body as I realized what they were grinning about. They all gathered close around me in a group hug. Kyle was against my ear.

I could hear him whispering through his tears, "You prayed in the Spirit, Ember. You did it."

I just nodded with my head in my hands and wept at the wonder of it all.

Slowly, our group made their way back to their seats. I wasn't ready to go yet. There were still people around the front of the church. I walked up to the bottom stair and knelt. Truthfully, I had never felt this much peace and joy in my life; I didn't want to leave. I knelt there and just soaked in the feeling and tried to express my gratitude, but could only come up with a feeble attempt. Occasionally, a person would walk by and touch my shoulder or back and say a soft prayer for me. After a few minutes, someone draped a blanket over my shoulders. It alarmed me because I thought it must be late. I reached back to hold it as I stood, but nothing was there. I looked around but no one was near either. Church was over so I walked back to say goodbye to my new friends. They couldn't stand the idea of my taking a taxi home and insisted on driving me.

❦

The next morning, I woke up with a start, a mixture of emotions racing through me as I sat straight up in bed. My heart pounded in my chest as I stared up at my closed door, waiting. The familiarity of Mom's singing and the roar of her coffee grinder helped calm me. The fact Mom was still there let me know it was early. I knew I had time to think. I allowed the thoughts of the previous night's events flood in as I lay back down in bed and stared at my blue ceiling.

At my request, my new friends had dropped me off at the crossroads down my street. It had been a quiet drive, with each person still relishing in the events of the night. They all hugged me as I got out of the car, though. We had shared something special, and it somehow seemed to bring us close. I ran all the way home, grinning until I got to the house and reality hit me. With sadness overtaking me, I sulked to the back of the house to climb in the window. I had propped open the screen with a stick and left my window cracked, a practice I had perfected years ago. With ease, I slithered into my window and quietly got dressed for bed by the light of my cell phone.

Now, I stared out that window feeling melancholy. It was unfair that all of the joy and peace I felt last night could dissipate so quickly because of a guilty conscience and another stupid dream. Something tickled at the edge of my mind. I stood up and paced my room, trying to remember what brought on such an intense reaction this morning. Something was different. Then, I gasped as I remembered. It was different. For the first time ever, my nightmare had deviated from the usual path. It played out in my mind as I stopped in the middle of the room, eyes focusing on nothing. It was the same; my room, the walls falling, the darkness and screams, and my cowering in fear, all happened like usual. Instead of the dream ending, there was a flash of light, so bright I saw it through my tightly squeezed eyes. Curiosity won over my fear and I opened my eyes a crack to see a shining silver sword lying on the floor beside me. I just stared at it for a while, still cowering from the wailing around me. Surely, whatever was causing all of that torment would make its way to me soon. But then I, the dream me, did something I didn't expect; she slowly reached down and with a sweaty hand, grabbed the sword. It seemed to strengthen her resolve somehow because once it was in her hand, she straightened herself up and walked slowly to the edge of her room. Then, with only a second of hesitation, she walked out into the darkness.

I was snapped back into the present at that point. I reached up to my face to find it wet with tears. I didn't know what it meant, but somehow I was proud of that person in the dream. That she finally made the decision to face her fear.

A decision that would more than likely get her killed, I thought as a shudder ran over me.

I looked back to my window and another pang of guilt hit me. I grabbed a tissue and dried my face then walked out of my room with the determination of my dream self.

"Hey, sleepyhead," Mom chided cheerfully as I walked into the kitchen. "I was afraid I would have to leave for work before I got the chance to see you."

Her happy mood made my resolve falter a bit. Maybe my confession could wait. I pushed that thought back and sat down at the table by Mom. I tried to look her in the eyes, but couldn't manage to look up from my feet.

With a shaky voice I began, "Mom, I've been awake in my room for a while. I didn't come out here right away because..."

"Because it's summer break and you're a teenager who has no life, blah, blah, blah," Mom interrupted and then actually laughed at the surprised look I gave her.

She wasn't even close, not this time. I turned in the chair and watched as she put her cup in the dishwasher.

"I really don't have to get into all of that this morning, Ember. Not if I'm going to have time to..."

I didn't let her finish. She was about to walk out the door and I knew I would never work up the courage to tell her about last night again. Even worse, she might hear about it through the gossips at work.

In a panic, I blurted, "I snuck out last night!"

At first, I wasn't sure she heard me. She slowly slid in the dishwasher rack, reached down for the door and closed it. My heart was hammering in my chest as she turned and leaned against the cabinet with feigned calm. I knew it was fake. Her death grip on the edge of countertop, white knuckles and all, gave her away. I bit my lip and waited for the wrath of her anger. Instead, there was only hurt in her voice.

She asked in barely a whisper, "How could you, Ember? I had hoped things would be different when we got you away from those girls, but you haven't changed a bit."

I know she didn't realize the power of those words, but they cut like razors to expose my real fear, that in spite of my best efforts, I couldn't escape the horrible things I had done in my past. I was still that terrible person. I had planned to just apologize for sneaking out, but there was so much regret in me that had been building for four years that there were no words to voice the sorrow I felt, only sobs. I felt Mom's arms around me as she knelt by my chair. Her love and humility made me cry even harder. She gently pushed my tear-soaked hair from my face and left. A couple of minutes later, she was back with tissues. As I cleaned up my face, she whispered how much she loved me and always would, no matter what mistakes I made. I was so relieved to know that she understood my grief. Then, she started making comments about young love and Cade. I had to interrupt.

"Whoa, wait a minute, Mom," I said, getting up to throw away the used tissues. "This has nothing to do with Cade."

She got up and sat in my vacant chair and waited for me to continue; obviously that was not what she was expecting to hear.

I let out a sigh and continued, "I snuck out last night to go to church."

"To church," she echoed numbly. "Then why all of the tears?" she asked after I nodded. "Did something bad happen?"

I couldn't stop the grin from spreading across my face as I

told her about the amazing service. I wasn't able to give any details because she interrupted, clearly not interested.

"Wait, you went to church last night and you feel guilty because..." she asked, trying to understand why I was so upset.

I thought a minute about trying to explain my real distress, but decided to keep it simple.

"Because," I continued for her, "I should have asked you. I was wrong and I'm sorry."

I still couldn't make eye contact with her and felt the tears threatening again. *Would I ever be a good person?* Once again, Mom walked to me with tears in her eyes.

"You *are* different, Ember. I'm sorry I haven't noticed it before. I just keep thinking you're making the same mistakes over and over, but you're not, are you?"

I assumed it was a rhetorical question so I remained quiet as she continued.

"You would have never confessed to sneaking out. I don't think you ever gave it a second thought all of those times you did it before. Don't look so surprised." She leaned back on the cabinet, continuing, "I'm not totally oblivious. I was concerned and went to Bill to talk to him about your behavior. He said it was just part of growing up and I should just let you have your fun." She gave me a sad smile. "I can't blame it all on Bill, though. I was busy with my new life, too, and just really didn't have the time to deal with what was going on with you. You were just a kid, but we just let you live your life with no real rules, no boundaries. I'm so sorry, Ember."

Then she pushed away from the counter and gave me a hug. In a lighter tone, she said, "But, that is all in the past now, isn't it? We're starting out with a clean slate. You are going to have rules, but I am going to trust you to follow them, OK?"

When I said I understood, she continued, "I know I've never been a good role model as far as religion goes." She held up her hand when I tried to object. "No, it's true. I've never stopped you from going to church and tried to find a way for you to get there when you were young, but we never went together. That may change now that you have that cute youth pastor."

"Ugh, Mom…!" I exclaimed with exaggerated disgust.

She laughed. "Seriously, Ember. Unless there is a very good reason, like sickness or big exams you need to study for, you'll always be allowed to go to church, OK? No more sneaking out, though."

I agreed and gave her a hug. I felt her tense as she stepped back and gave an exasperated sigh.

"Ugh! The time! I was going to do this with a little more pomp and circumstance," Mom said as she grabbed her keys and hooked her arm around mine and bounced toward the carport.

I laughed at her silliness, but let myself be led, full of curiosity now.

"*Ta-da!*" she exclaimed with a swipe of her arm.

"A car!" I yelped. "You got me a car!"

Parked in the carport was a little red four-door sedan. It was a beautiful sight! It was my turn to bounce now. I grabbed her around the shoulders and jumped up and down, giggling. I was still grinning as she handed me the keys.

"But, Mom, how can we afford it? Did Bill help?"

She patted my cheek with a smile. "Well, it's used, but with very few miles. Our new mechanic told me about it and checked everything out for me before I bought it. Even he said it was a great deal. And, in a way, Bill helped," Mom replied as she stepped out toward the street.

I followed her out and saw a car almost identical to mine in the driveway, only silver instead of red.

"We match," she added with a smile.

Realization hit me, leaving a lump in my throat. "You traded in your Mercedes," I said, my excitement deflating at the thought of her sacrifice. She walked back to me for another quick hug.

"Oh, honey, don't feel bad. You needed a car and I definitely did not need a new Mercedes. It sticks out like a sore thumb around here."

She waited until I gave her a nod. Satisfied, Mom got into her car. After it was cranked, she rolled down the window and waited for me to walk over.

"I know you have your learner's permit, but I want to give you a little refresher course before you drive without me, all right? I'll see if I can switch shifts with someone so we can go get your license soon. I put a test booklet in the glove compartment."

Once again, I nodded. She drove away, leaving me staring at my new keys. This was definitely not how I'd imagined this morning would end up. I tossed up the keys and caught them with a grin.

"Not in my wildest dreams," I said to no one. Then, I walked back to check out my new car.

I had just unlocked it when I heard the phone ringing inside. Frustrated, I gave one last, loving look to my car then ran inside to answer it. It was Cade. He was just warming up with his lecture about my not answering my cell phone when I screamed the news in his ear.

"Your Mom got you wheels!" he yelled over my squeals of delight.

"Yes!" I exclaimed, jumping up and down in the kitchen.

"I'm coming over to see it!" he said, bringing my giddiness to an abrupt halt.

"No! Don't even think about it," I began.

"I'm just kidding," he reassured. "Just text me a photo of you and her together, and I'll be satisfied...for now," he added in usual Cade fashion. I guess all was forgiven.

I reached up and felt my still-damp hair, then looked down at my pajamas and bare feet before replying, "Um, I'll send it in a few. Talk to you later!"

I did send Cade the photo but much later, after an email to Vie, a phone call to Missy, a shower and change of clothes, and a very long time behind the wheel of my new, parked car.

Chapter Seven

T HE NEXT FEW days went by in a blur of driving lessons and traffic rules. Mom was true to her word and gave me a refresher course, while Missy and Cade did their part by acting as tutors. Violet couldn't be there, of course, but supported me by being just as delighted as I was at the prospect of being able to drive. Driving cross-country to see all of the sights we had read about as kids was something we had both dreamt about since we were little. It still made me a little heartsick to think about how far we were apart. She was extremely happy that I had spent time with Granny. I promised that once I got my license, I would see Granny again. I didn't realize at the time just how soon that visit would take place. I didn't know that upsetting events would lead to my mad dash to her house, either. Had I known, I would have tried to get my license that Tuesday.

"Aww, no. Seriously?" I asked whining.

"I'm sorry, Ember. I should've called to check their hours. I just assumed it would be open on Monday," Mom replied, frustrated, as she backed the car out of the lot.

I was already on the phone dialing Missy. She made me

promise I would call her as soon as I knew anything. "The stupid place is closed," I grumbled as soon as she answered. "All of my worrying for nothing."

She tried to make me feel better by suggesting I try again tomorrow. Unfortunately, Mom wouldn't be able to switch shifts for a while, so I might not get another chance until after school began. I felt like crying when I explained it to Missy. She told me to hold on a minute. I rested my head on the cool window and watched trees pass by as I waited.

"I can take you tomorrow," she said happily.

"Really? I thought you had to work all this week," I replied hopefully.

"I just told Mom about it and she said it wasn't a problem." I thanked Missy and her mother about a hundred times on the way home.

The next morning, Missy pulled into the same spot Mom and I had sat in the day before. My stomach was full of butter-flies again, possibly more. I had called to make sure they were open this time. Missy squeezed my hand, calming my nerves a little. I smiled and asked if she would be OK waiting. She had insisted earlier that it was too far away to make the drive home and back. Once again, she assured me she would be fine. We walked into the little brick building. My face fell when I saw the small seating area was already half full with people waiting their turns, small white numbers in their hands. We were only ten minutes late. With a sigh, I went to sign in and get a number while Missy scouted us out two orange, plastic chairs in the corner to sit. We didn't talk; I was too nervous and she was, well...Missy, but just having someone with me helped my frazzled nerves. Finally, they called my number and I jumped up. Missy gave me a quick hug and told me she would be at the flea market across the street. I nodded and nervously made my way to the test room.

What seemed to be hours later, I walked, elated, out of the building staring at my new license. I had to look up for a minute to cross the road, but quickly turned my gaze back to the small ticket to freedom in my hand. It hurt when I ran into that pole. Missy erupted into laughter, drawing my attention.

"Are you all right?" she asked, suppressing her giggles so she could check my head without doing more damage.

I just grinned and showed her my license.

"You're going to look great in your car, bump and all," she joked.

We laughed and turned to go back across the street to the car. The flea market only opened for the morning on Tuesdays and Thursdays so it was mostly deserted now, giving the place an eerie feel. I was about to say so to Missy, when I saw the man. He was wearing what looked to be a camouflage jacket and pants, but was tattered with holes and covered in what probably was months of grime. His beard was tangled and his long, greasy hair hung limply down his back. The man was sitting in the dirt, legs sprawled out in front of him, with an empty bottle lying beside him. His elbow was on a table behind him in a vacant stall and his filthy hand was covering his face. My feet were locked in place. Living in the city, I had seen homeless people before and this man didn't seem any different. I was different this time. I could hear the confusion in Missy's voice as she tried to encourage me to come with her, but even when she started to plead, I couldn't follow. Instead, I started walking toward the man.

"Ember," she hissed, "What are you doing? That guy is obviously drunk and no telling what else," she added while tugging on my sleeve.

She frantically looked around us, as if to find some help, but it did no good. The few stragglers had left and I was determined to talk to the man anyway. It was only when she yelled, "Stop!" that I actually paid attention to her.

"What?" I asked frustrated. "The guy is obviously too whacked to be able to do me any real harm, Missy."

She rolled her eyes at my argument. "Look, if you want to help him, we'll give some money for Pastor Eric to give to him. I mean, from the looks of him, I don't think he'll be going anywhere for a while."

Although we were too far away for the man to hear us, he slowly turned to look at us. Missy let out a panicked squeak, making her sound like her namesake.

"I am just going to talk to him, Missy," I said slowly while peeling her hand off my arm. "I know he looks bad, but..."

"But, what?" she asked, frustration showing in her voice.

I ran my hands through my hair to push it out of my face and turned around, giving myself time before facing her again. "It wasn't his fault, Missy. He needs to know that."

"What are you talking about, Ember?" she questioned me, probably relieved I had some excuse for my madness.

"He was in the Vietnam War, Missy and saw two of his best friends die, shot in front of him," I cringed at the memory. "He thinks it was his fault, but..."

"How do you know?" Missy bellowed.

Coming from her it was practically a scream, so I knew she was freaked out. In truth, I didn't know how I knew, I just did. How could I possibly explain that, though? I couldn't, so instead I just stared at her blankly. She just shook her head and walked away.

"Fine. If you don't want to tell me, don't, but I'm getting out of here. He's still staring at us and it's giving me the creeps."

I looked over again at the man, my emotions torn and confused. His bloodshot eyes didn't give me any clues about his past as he stared at me. They were too dull from alcohol. I almost walked over to him then, but the need for a ride won over my desire to talk to him; besides, maybe I was totally off base. I grudgingly broke eye contact with him and took off in a slow jog to catch up with Missy.

Missy didn't mention the man when I drove her home. In fact, she didn't say much of anything. Normally, I would have just blown it off as her personality, but I knew better. She was still very upset that I wouldn't level with her. I thanked her again when I dropped her off, then stopped by Mom's work to let her know I had passed the test. There were a lot of hugs and congratulations for me from all of the staff. I hope that no one sensed my lingering unease.

On the way home, I went over what happened at the market repeatedly, but things just didn't add up. How could I have known those things about that man? I didn't even tell Missy the whole truth of it. I saw everything. It was like a movie playing in my head. I couldn't explain it, but I couldn't deny that it was real, either. And the way I was determined to walk right up to a strange, drunk man. I normally wouldn't have done that in a million years, and I had done some crazy things in the past. I pulled up onto our carport and switched off the car. Just like that, it was like another switch had turned on in my brain. It felt just like my dream. I had the same kind of determination as in my dream. My nightmare never changed...until after the service Wednesday night. I jumped out of the car and went straight to my room to find Kyle's phone number.

I held my breath while his cell phone rang, over and over, praying that he would answer. Finally, right before being sent to voice mail, he picked up. "Hello," Kyle said, slightly out of breath. I let mine out in a rush of relief and told him it was me. He seemed genuinely happy to hear from me and explained that it took a while for him to find his phone under all the piles in his bedroom. It made me feel much better about the mess in my room. I heard someone, I think it was his mother, tell him it was time to go. Kyle assured me he had some time. So, with a warning that I might be insane, I gave him an abbreviated version of what had happened to me that morning.

Instead of fear, I heard awe in his voice, "Wow, Ember! That sounds like..." someone, his dad this time, interrupted again. "Sorry, I have to go, but it sounds like you were using the gift of knowledge."

"Huh?"

"The gift of knowledge. It's one of the gifts of the Spirit. I'm not sure, but you might have it. I have to go. Just do some research on it and let me know. If you have it, you can totally read people's mail. Cool."

With that great wisdom, we hung up. I hoped he got out the door without being in too much trouble with his parents.

The strange experience with the homeless man and the exhilaration of finally having a car and license was put on hold due to the upcoming back to school party our youth group was planning. I got plenty of practice driving, but unfortunately, I only spent the time driving between home, church, and the grocery store to work on the party and to buy supplies. Missy seemed to have forgiven me, or at least decided to forget what happened. When Thursday rolled around, I was quite surprised to be woken up, bright and early, by the doorbell. I groaned and looked at my cell phone by my bed. It was too early to be awake. I knew Mom hadn't left for work yet, so I buried my head under my pillow and tried to go back to sleep. It was not to be.

"Ember," Mom called in a singsong voice, as she popped her head into my room.

"What," I groaned.

"You have some visitors," was her reply.

I snatched the pillow off my head, sat up in shock and mouthed, "Who?"

She just smiled and opened my door all the way. Two people flew by Mom and landed in the middle of my bed.

"Happy Freedom Day!" Missy and Cade yelled in unison.

It took me a second to realize it was Thursday. My restriction was over. I knew I had a terrible case of bed-head, but I didn't care. Mom had already slipped out of my room so the coast was clear. I stood up and started dancing on the bed. Missy ran over and turned on my stereo, and then they both joined me in my victory dance.

After we settled down, Missy and Cade helped themselves to cereal while I got dressed. Then we piled into my car (Missy called shotgun) and we spent the morning cruising around in my car. I had made a special playlist for just such an occasion, so we were all hoarse from singing by the time I dropped Missy off at work before the lunch rush. Cade opened the door for Missy and walked her in. A few minutes later, he came back and took her place by me.

"Should I take you home now?" I asked backing away from the cafeteria.

"Not a chance," Cade said, holding up a bag.

From the delicious smells coming from the brown bag, I knew he must have snagged some food for us. With a laugh, I pulled back into the space then backed out again, this time toward our lake.

⁂

"That was delicious," Cade said.

"And too much," I added, as I laid a hand on my full stomach. "I have to remember to keep a picnic blanket in my trunk," I thought aloud.

"It's OK. The grass is soft."

I just nodded and laid back, content to be quiet and stare at the fluffy, white clouds as they blew past us. The wind had picked up, making it tolerable where we were, on a little hill above the lake. There were a few other couples and families swimming and playing in the water. Their presence made me feel much more relaxed around Cade. I heard him lay back beside me with a sigh. We stayed that way for a long time, until he broke the silence.

"Ember," he began.

I turned my head and saw he was lying on his side looking at me intently so I waited for the rest.

After a long minute of silence, he rolled back again. "Nothing," he said, sounding frustrated.

I rolled to my side and propped my head up on my arm. My heart gave a little leap, looking at him lying there. I had forgotten just how handsome he was. He reached up and ran his hand through my hair, staring at the sunshine through it as it fell back across my face. The next time, he moved it behind my shoulder, and then ran his hand down my neck. I shivered at his light touch, then quickly moved to sit up.

"I'm so glad we're friends, Cade," I said smiling down at him. "Really," I added, "I don't know what I would have done this summer without our friendship."

Cade didn't respond. Instead he sat up, too, crossing his arms across his knees. "What's been going on with you lately, Em?" he asked, still looking out toward the lake.

That certainly wasn't what I expected him to say.

"I don't know what you mean."

"Mouse told me," he paused before continuing, "she told me about the homeless man, Ember. You really scared her."

"What?" I asked, my voice rising. "That was nothing. I just wanted to talk to a guy for a second. I can't believe she made such a big deal..."

"She didn't make a big deal about it."

"Really, then why did she even bother telling you?" I demanded.

I didn't wait for him to reply; instead, I started cleaning up from our picnic. I needed something to do with my hands.

"Ember, would you cool down for a minute? It wasn't a big deal, but now, with the way you're acting..."

I cut him a look of warning.

"You're acting all defensive and angry and I haven't even finished what I was going to say. You see, that's not like you," he added softly as he touched my arm.

He was right. I was angry, but madder at myself than anyone was. I told him so.

"So, you wanted to help the homeless guy but didn't because Missy was scared and you're angry because of that?" he asked.

I finished putting our garbage in the bag while I thought of what to say. How would I even begin? And, could I be honest with him? I put down the bag and sat on my knees, facing Cade. He smiled in response, knowing instinctively that I was going to confess something, though I'm sure he would never have guessed what I was about to say. I hadn't even truly admitted it to myself.

"Cade," I began, "I wanted to talk to the homeless guy because I knew something that could help him, I think. The guy was a mess because of something that happened in his past." I looked away now. "If anyone knows about past regrets, it's me."

"That's ridiculous, Ember. You're one of the nicest people..."

"I haven't always been nice."

"You've said that before, but..."

Cade must have realized I wasn't budging, because he changed the subject.

"OK, look, whatever. You say you were a terrible person. You were a terrible person. Happy?"

I just shrugged.

Cade rolled his eyes and began again, "So you knew something that you thought would help him."

"Yeah." I sat back and crossed my legs. I started picking random pieces of grass, trying to avoid the ants. "I knew he had a lot of guilt about the war, from some of his friends dying. I thought it would help him to know what really happened. That it wasn't his fault they died."

Cade reached over and put his hand on mine, stopping me so I would turn to him. "That was nice of you, Ember. But how do you know that about his friends? Was that guy a relative you recognized or something? Why wouldn't you tell Mouse? That was why she was so freaked out, you know. You just clammed up on her."

I let out a deep breath and stood up. Cade had to shade his eyes from the sun to see me, so I walked under the tree and leaned against it, looking down as I kicked at the dirt. "That's the funny part, Cade. I don't know how I know."

I looked at him to see his reaction. He stood up and slapped the grass off his pants. Walking toward me, he asked, "So, like amnesia or something? Your memory is starting to come back?"

"No, Cade. It's like..." I kicked at the dirt again, trying to come up with some explanation that wouldn't make me seem like a total lunatic. "It's like when you are trying to remember a name, um, like of an artist of a song. You know?"

"OK," he answered, standing in front of me.

I felt caged in with my back against the tree so I walked around him.

"It's like when you go around all day, racking your brain for this person's name, then suddenly, like from thin air..."

"It just drops in," he finished for me.

I turned toward him, grinning now. "Exactly! It's like it's been there all along, somewhere in your brain. And when you stop trying or least expect it, the name just kind of 'downloads.' That's what it was like when I knew about this guy, Cade. It just kind of dropped into my brain, like I had always known."

"But Ember, with the forgotten name, I would have known it before and just remembered at a weird time. There is no way you could have known that stuff about that homeless guy, so where did the information come from?"

"God?" I croaked, questioning my own sanity. I cleared my throat and tried again, "Maybe God gave me some kind of ability to know things." I bit my lip and waited, unable to turn around and face him.

"*God*, Ember?" he asked in disbelief. "What are these church freaks feeding you? They're telling you that you can read minds, that you're some kind of clairvoyant?"

I looked at him now as he ran his hand through his hair in frustration. He slapped his hand down on his leg and shook his head at me.

"You know what? For someone who is supposed to know things," he spat out bitterly, "you sure are clueless."

I knew then Cade was the last person I should have said

anything to about this. I deserved his anger; what else could I expect from him? Belief? I drew myself up from my slouch and faced him head on, letting my anger show. I wanted to get this over.

"What, Cade? I'm clueless about what?" I demanded.

He hesitated as if deciding whether to continue. He walked up to me, coming so close our bodies almost touched.

"I don't believe you have some special ability to know things, Ember, because if you did…if you did, you would know that I'm not your friend, Ember. I am in love with you; one hundred percent, head over heels, in love with you. But I am tired of being pushed away. I'm done, Ember."

Cade turned away from me in disgust. I heard him on his phone asking someone for a ride as he stomped away. I stayed there under the tree for a long time watching him go, but he didn't look back.

I stood there until I convinced myself he wasn't coming back. With resignation, I finished cleaning up our stuff and drove home. I was proud of myself. I stayed calm the whole drive home, only letting the flood of tears go when I was in my room. When no tears were left, I desperately wanted to talk to someone, so I prayed for a while. Then, I decided to write Violet, hoping she could bring some of her calm wisdom into my weird situation.

I padded my way down the hall, discarding a handful of used tissues as I went by the bathroom to our office. Mom must have turned on the computer this morning because it came on when I touched the mouse. She had been looking at the local news. I gasped when I saw the front page. It was a photo of the home-less man. It was obviously an old photo, because he was neat and smiling, but it was definitely him. The headline read that he was dead, apparently by suicide. I didn't think about what to do next. I just put on my shoes, scribbled a note to Mom, and went straight to my car.

By the time I arrived at the little house, it was nearing sunset. Once again, I stayed calm on the drive, but my hands started shaking so badly once I stopped that I could barely get the key out of the ignition. Thankfully, there were no more tears. I walked onto the flower-drenched porch and knocked. I was so happy to see Mrs. Denton; I almost hugged her, but she beat me to it. After the long hug, she released me and invited me in. I asked right away if I could see Granny. She had to have thought my request to see Granny was strange, but she didn't say so. Instead, she nodded and told me to follow her back.

"Granny, you have a visitor," Mrs. Denton said as she walked through the back bedroom door.

I waited just outside until Mrs. Denton waved me in. There wasn't much in the little room. Only a tall dresser with a lamp and a few photo frames, a chair, a lace curtain that blew with the window unit's cold air, and a blue oval rug on the floor by an automatic bed, like the ones in the hospital. I walked over to Granny and took her small, outstretched hand. Mrs. Denton let us know she would be in the kitchen making dinner. After I assured her I wouldn't be staying to eat, she quietly slipped out and closed the door with a small click.

"It's good to see you again, sweetheart," said Granny in a weak voice, but I knew she meant it. Her smile said so. "Tell Granny everything," she said, removing her hand from mine then folding both in her lap.

I nodded. I managed to tell her about the homeless man and about how my friends treated me, all without crying. Then, I got to the part about his death. She reached out to me. I collapsed in her lap and cried while she stroked my hair. Granny didn't say anything until I finished crying tears that I didn't think I had left to cry. She gave me some tissues and waited patiently for me to compose myself again.

"God chooses to do His work through people. He sent His Son down here through one. Everyone always blames the darkness in this world on God, but people allowed it. You understand me?" she asked, directing her steely gaze at me.

I thought back to my early lessons about Adam and Eve in the Garden of Eden and nodded, not wanting to speak, but to learn all I could from this woman of God.

"For whatever the reason, and I won't question the infinite wisdom of God, He has chosen us simple folk to battle it, the darkness. And He gave us the Holy Spirit to guide us, along with gifts of the Spirit. We use those gifts to point the lost and hurting to Jesus. That's why they're called *signs* and wonders," she added with a chuckle. We are saved by grace, that amazing free gift of God, that even after all my years, still boggles this brain," Granny said pointing to her head. "But for me, I don't just want a free ride to heaven, honey. I want everyone to have this precious gift of salvation, so one day they all can get there too. I want to fight the darkness while I'm still here. But it takes warriors, Christians who aren't afraid to fight. The Holy Spirit has given us the tools to make a difference. You remember that little song you learned in church, about 'this little light of mine'?" she asked.

Once again, I nodded, smiling at the memory.

"The Light of the World is in here," she said, tapping my chest.

It sounded wonderful. I wanted to jump and start helping people right then and there, but then I remembered Cade's face as he spat out hateful words to me, wounding me. I whispered, "I feel like I'm alone, though. If I start telling people that I hear God, they'll probably lock me away. My friends don't even believe me and one of them is a Christian. I felt tears stinging my eyes again and reached out to be reassured by Granny. I got something else instead, what I didn't want to hear.

"Yes, you will be made fun of, yelled at, and probably more. So was our Lord and Savior; but count it all joy, honey. You will have your reward. I promise," she added more gently. "Sweetheart, the disciples were made fun of when they came down from that Upper Room; everyone thought they were drunker than skunks," she said with a laugh. "They said horrible things about those people who visited Azusa Street, but you know what? The thing that was happening, it was bigger than that Upper Room, bigger than that little revival on that little street; and what's happening with you, little girl, is much bigger than what you can ever imagine. You have been given an amazing gift," Granny said, as she grabbed my hand. "Use it for His glory, honey. Show the ones who are sick, lost, and hurting the signs and wonders. They will know where they truly came from and they will rejoice in Him. Pick up your sword," she continued even as my head snapped up and my eyes bulged, "pick it up and fight the good fight."

With that, Granny laid back and fell asleep, stopping all of my questions with a snap of her eyelids. With a sigh, I quietly left her room to say my goodbyes to Mrs. Denton.

A full-sized Delorean model hung from the ceiling with assorted colored lights flashing off its silver body in time with the thumping sounds of the music. We had been planning this party for weeks. I had been grateful for the distraction the previous day. Even Missy had seemed shaken and extremely tender around me yesterday after hearing the news about the homeless man. I looked around at all of the food and decorations. I had obviously never grasped just how amazing the outcome of all of our planning and work would be. It must have been just a test run, because all of the music and party lights shut down and the main lights were turned on just in time for me to spot Missy heading my way.

"Isn't it amazing? Your clothes are just perfect, by the way."

"That was my exact thought when I walked in; amazing," I agreed. "And thanks," I added.

The theme for the dance was "Back to School" but with a *Back to the Future* feel. One of the work groups made the car from the movie. We chose the 80s as the time warp era. I had "big" hair, big earrings, bright red lips, and neon pink leg warmers to match my neon green shirt. At least no one would run over me if I decided to go for a walk. Missy looked cute in her tutu and wild hair; she had a Cindy Lauper vibe going. Before I could compliment her, Pastor Eric interrupted. He told us we did a great job, cleared up a few questions, and then said a quick prayer. Then, it was time. We all took our places as the party lights and music started back up. I was on first shift to help with refreshments so I made my way to the concession stand just as kids started piling into the auditorium.

It was after 11:00 before the last of the partiers made their way out and the doors were locked. The lights came on and those of us remaining for cleanup duty looked around at the mess in horror. Once again, Pastor Eric was there for encouragement. Thankfully, the dozen or so of us didn't have to clean everything; there would be a crew coming in for that; we just needed to clean off the tables and toss all of the garbage. With our load lightened, the music came back on and we began singing, dancing, and working. It actually turned out to be a lot of fun. I was singing along to "Beat It" and folding up a table when Reid offered to help. I gladly accepted his help. He picked up the heavy table with ease so I could fold up the legs. Maybe it was exhaustion, but a silly thought crossed my mind and made me giggle. Reid moved the table to the wall, then asked what was so funny. I tried to blow it off, but after he tortured me with a few tickles, I was toast.

... "OK, OK, just stop tickling me," I laughed as I pushed him away. He just stared at me and tapped his foot expectantly. "This is so going to give you the big head, but fine." I rolled my eyes then blurted out, "I was thinking that you're very strong and then it occurred to me that you kind of look like that guy on TV who plays Superman, you know with your dark hair and blue eyes...so I couldn't help but picture you in tights..."

I yelped as he grabbed at me and continued to run around the auditorium to get away from more torture. Reid's friends stood talking in a group, now finished with their work tasks. I figured there was safety in numbers so I ran over and crouched behind another one of the guys on the football team. The rat dragged me out from my hiding place. "You looking for her?" asked the traitor. "Yes, I was, in fact, looking for just that person," said Reid with a smirk on his face.

I closed my eyes with dread and saw him. I saw Reid and I knew what was going on with him. I opened my eyes and whispered, "Stop." There must have been something in my voice to let the group know I was serious. All of the laughing stopped. They formed a circle around the two of us and were looking at me curiously. I thought about keeping my mouth shut. I did. Then, the newspaper article about that man—I knew I couldn't risk that kind of outcome again. I thought about Granny and her words of encouragement the day before, and then I told them what I knew. I spoke directly to Reid, but they all heard. When I finished, you could hear a pin drop. The music that had been blaring earlier was silent. There was only silence until Reid spoke up.

"You're crazy," he said in a deadly serious voice. "I don't know where you heard that, but it's not true."

With those words he, and everyone else, turned and walked toward the door. When Reid reached the exit, he turned and threatened, "You had better never repeat those lies to anyone."

He looked at the others with him until each of them agreed. Finally, he looked back at me like he wanted to say more. He probably wanted to threaten me with bodily harm, but there were still some adults around somewhere. Instead, they all just left me standing by myself until I couldn't endure the embarrassment any longer. Pastor Eric found me on the floor, rocking back and forth with my head in my hands—a position that no longer seemed to be just for nightmares.

It was Sunday and Mom was home. Thankfully, she hadn't bothered me this morning, although it had to be noon by then. I just couldn't face anyone, not after last night. Pastor Eric had been very kind. I didn't tell him anything; I just let him assume I was having guy troubles, which wasn't too far from the truth. I heard Mom's keys jingle and the door close so I got up to sneak a look out of the front window just in time to see her drive away. A note on the fridge let me know she was going into town to buy me a few things from my school supply list. A pang of guilt hit me when I realized she probably would have wanted me to go. Hopefully, she thought I was still tired from the party last night. I guess that was true, too. I didn't get home until well after midnight. I looked back at the note and felt my stomach drop. The first day of school was tomorrow. I had actually been looking forward to it, back when I had friends. Saddened, I moped back into my room, crawled under my covers, and slept.

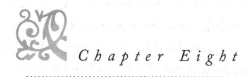

Chapter Eight

"EMBER, ARE YOU ready? You don't want to miss your first day of school," Mom yelled from the kitchen.

"Oh yes I do," I replied under my breath as I put on my third coat of mascara.

It was overkill, I know, but I still wasn't ready to see all of those people yet. Missy hadn't even called me yesterday. Everyone must know about it now, even Cade. I cringed at the thought. He would really think I had gone off the deep end.

"Emb..."

"I'm coming!" I yelled back, before she could finish the thought. With one last glance in the mirror, I left my room to start my first day as a junior and a freak of nature.

The first week at my new school was terrible, but in a surprisingly normal way; I got lost constantly, humiliated in P.E. by multiple sports-related goofs, and ate my sandwich in the bathroom at lunch instead of facing a sea of unfamiliar faces in the cafeteria. In spite of all of the pain, I was still grateful that it wasn't worse. Missy seemed to have forgiven me, once again, if she even knew about the Reid incident. By the looks of pity I saw her give me when she didn't think I was looking, I would guess that she definitely knew, but kept quiet; yet another thing to be grateful for.

Reid and his friends, on the other hand, never looked my way at all. They completely ignored me, going so far as to walk on the other side of the hall from me. Cade was the hardest one to deal with because he was somewhere between the two extremes, trying very hard to ignore me, but failing miserably. Even walking toward me like he had every intention to talk to me, then turning away from me completely; leaving me standing there with a fading smile, alone in my confusion. I couldn't get a word about him from Missy. I would try to ask nonchalantly how Cade was doing, but would only get the silent treatment in return. Like I said, it was terrible, but at least there were no more "downloads" about people. Even the nightmares had been happening less frequently lately. You would think I would be happy, but instead I just existed, with a gaping hole inside of me.

I spent the next weeks of school leading that kind of existence, trying not to upset the balance of things, and never being truly happy with the status quo. It was fall and though things stayed mostly green, the air did get cooler and scarecrows and blow up turkeys started taking the place of ghouls and jack-o-lanterns in yards.

"Do you have any plans tonight?"

Lately, Mom had been asking that question often. By the way she bit her lip, I knew she was hoping for a different response this time.

"No, I think I'm going to stay home and get a head start on my midterms."

"But, Ember, it's Friday night. Don't you want to go to the football game?"

"No!" I snapped out, a little too harshly. It was getting harder to keep up the façade of normalcy. I was cracking under the pressure of my mother to get a life.

"Well, then what if we go to the Fall Festival in town tomorrow? Certainly, you'll be tired of studying by then. Besides, we won't stay long," she said with finality.

My weekend was doomed to be spent at home studying and shopping for local crafts in handmade booths. I think my bad behavior should be excused, the tossing of my plate in the sink and stomping out of the room. I slammed my door and flung myself across the bed. This should not be my life.

"Well, then, I'm going to the game…if you're sure you don't want to come along." After a moment of heavy silence, she let out a sigh and gave up. I heard her drive away a few minutes later.

I couldn't stand the thought that my mother had more of a life than I did, so I picked up the phone and called Missy. I only got her voicemail. She was probably at the game anyway, something I could never do, as long as Reid was the quarterback. The memory I had of him, the one I shouldn't have known, came back but I quickly clamped it back down and started getting ready for a night out.

I drove slowly by the stadium with my window down, in spite of the chilly air. I could hear the roar of the crowd and smell the popcorn. I had always loved football when I was a cheerleader at my old school. I shook my head to banish the thought, something I always seemed to be doing lately. Then, I noticed the light on my dash. I didn't want to pump gas in the cold, but it looked like it was inevitable. I drove to the nearest station. It was an old one, so I had to pump then pay. I got enough gas to get me home, pulled up to a spot by the door, and ran inside to escape the cold. I said hi to the only other person there, the elderly attendant, and looked over the aisles for a snack.

"Why, hello Ember," a male voice said behind me.

I turned to find Cade's dad standing by me.

"You scared me, Mr. Malone. I didn't know anyone else was in here."

"I was just in the restroom trying to get some of the gas I spilt off my hands. I was just on my way home from work," he added with a smile that made my skin crawl.

I couldn't understand why this guy bothered me so, but didn't want to stick around to figure it out. I decided to forgo the snack and with a smile in return, left Mr. Malone to pay for my gas. He caught me again on the way out.

"Shouldn't you be at the game cheering on your team, Ember?"

"I just wasn't in the mood for company tonight," I said with a shrug, hoping to get my point across that I wanted to be alone. Obviously it didn't work because he smoothly blocked my way to the door by reaching out to hold the end of the aisle. I glanced over my shoulder for the attendant, but his back was turned to us as he watched the small black and white television.

"I hear you and my boy had a little falling out. Is that true?" he asked with a tilt of his head, still smiling that awful smile of his.

"I still consider Cade my friend," I retorted. "Now, it's getting late. I really should get going before my mom worries about me."

"Oh, she won't be worried. She went with my wife to the football game. Didn't you know?"

I didn't know how to answer that, so I didn't bother.

"I'll see you later, Mr. Malone," I announced and was ready to push my way past him if necessary. Instead, I froze as the awful truth about Mr. Malone hit me in full force.

"How could you?" I gasped. "How could you do that to your own daughter?" The horror of it almost took my breath away. Mr. Malone knew that I knew. I could see it in his face; the shock and a second of guilt flashed across his features before turning into a twisted mask of hatred.

"I don't know what you're talking about," he spat at me.

He threw a quick glance at the man behind the counter to make certain we weren't heard. Satisfied, he glared at me again, then abruptly turned and stormed out of the gas station. I pretended like I was looking at candy until I was sure he was gone, then I walked back and sat in my car, suddenly afraid to go home. Instead, I drove back to the stadium and parked. I huddled in my cold car, wrapped in my unused picnic blanket. I waited, trembling from the cold and from memories; empathizing with Cami's hatred for her father.

I was curled up watching TV when Mom got home from the game. She didn't know, but I made it in the door only a few minutes before she did. I had waited until the game was over before I dared to come home by myself. After she went to bed, I watched two movies before sleep deprivation finally won out over my panicked brain and I fell into a restless sleep.

I was still on the couch when Mom found me the next morning. She shoved away a pile of blankets to have room to sit by me. Even with the mountain of covers, it had taken hours for me to feel warm again last night. The crease between her eyes showed the concern she felt for me. I used the opportunity and claimed exhaustion to avoid going to the Fall Festival. It wasn't untrue.

"Honey, are you sure you don't want to get out for a while?"

"Mom, you saw yourself, I stayed up way too late watching movies last night. I just want to take a long shower and catch a nap. Really, I'm fine," I insisted, untangling myself from the blanket so I could make a quick exit.

"Ember, something is wrong and you're not telling me what's going on. That isn't like you, not anymore. Please, Ember," she pleaded, "I can even promise you up front that there will be no restriction, no matter what has happened. OK?"

"A get out of restriction free card?" I asked in disbelief. She must have been more worried than I thought.

"Ember, you have put yourself on a much stricter restriction lately than I ever would."

I stopped with a sigh and leaned back on the couch for a minute to think. I couldn't tell her everything. I thought of Cade's reaction again and shuddered involuntarily. She would have me committed. I had to tell her some of it, though. She didn't deserve this.

"OK, Mom. The truth is, I'm just having a really hard time fitting in here. Cade has kind of blown me off because I'm a Christian, and even Missy acts a little weird around me because I visited that other church and…" I glanced at Mom nervously. She was sitting sideways on the couch staring at the wall. I could tell she was tense, but she was handling it OK, so I continued. "…and, well, they believe some different things. Anyway, it's the kids at school, too. I mean, it's small, like everything around here, and they've all been friends forever. I think it's hard for them to let someone new in their groups. And then, there's my own personality crisis. I don't even know who I am anymore. It's like I was this person before and I hated who I was, but now I have a chance to be different but I don't know how to be," I finished, staring down at my hands. "Everything is just really screwed up right now."

Mom pulled me to her chest. "Why didn't you tell me you were having such a hard time?" she asked.

She had no idea just how hard it was.

"I didn't want you to regret your decision about moving us here. I know you want us to be happy and you seem to really like it here."

I felt her nod.

"I do. I like a small town, but if it's not right for you, we can look into other places."

She pulled me away from her so I could face her. "It's not worth it, Ember. I can't stand to see you locked away and alone all of the time. It's not like you." She gave me an abrupt nod and started to get up, her mind already set to move. I reached out and grabbed her hand.

"No, Mom, really. I'm OK. I want to stick it out here, at least until I graduate. I don't have that long, you know," I said, hoping I sounded more resolved than I felt.

She let go of my hand and gently patted my cheek. "We'll give it some more time, then. But I'm not going to just sit around and let you waste away." She turned to walk out, like a woman on a mission.

"Where are you going?" I asked anxiously.

"I'm going to meet Cade's mom at the festival like we had planned."

I slouched in relief, but it was too soon.

Right before Mom went out of the door she continued, "Then, I'm going to give her an earful about how badly her son has been treating my daughter." She was already driving away by the time I got the blasted blankets off me and ran out the front door to stop her.

Only hours later, Cade showed up on our doorstep with flowers for Mom and an apology for me. The flowers were colorful and smelled wonderful. The apology did not. Although it was painfully obvious the apology was coerced, I accepted, even asking him in for a visit. He declined, but before leaving, he handed Mom a note. She tore it open as I closed the door.

"A-ha!" she exclaimed. "I knew things would be right as rain again if we all just acted civilized. You and Cade have made up and we," she smiled, waving the card in front of me, "have been invited to the Malones' for Thanksgiving dinner."

My reaction spoke for me. Mom took one look at my face and got angry.

"No. Don't you even think about trying to worm your way out of this, young lady. They have done their part, and we are going to do ours. You. Are. Going."

※

Over the next two weeks, I was busy with midterms and preparing for the youth group's Thanksgiving lunch. It was held the Saturday before Thanksgiving and was a great success, not only in feeding the needy, but it was also successful in keeping my mind from the upcoming dinner at the Malones' house. Each time I thought about the hatred I had seen in Mr. Malone, I got sick to my stomach. There was no joy about seeing Cade, either. He had been civil to me at school, but things were still mostly the same between us—cold. Mom was happy, though. She was proud of herself for bringing us all back together. It was an erroneous belief, based on how busy I had become lately and the fact that I didn't put up any more arguments about the Malones. The truth was, Missy had let it slip that Cami would be there. The hope of seeing her quieted some of my dread. Maybe something good would come out of it after all.

We were late for dinner Thanksgiving evening. Mom hadn't approved of my outfit, sending me back to my room to change. I rolled my eyes at the irony of it. Only a few months earlier, she would have argued that I was showing too much of something. Now, when I came out fully covered, it wasn't good enough. Granted, the sweatshirt and jeans weren't exactly fancy, but...

"Ember, come on!" Mom yelled, interrupting my thoughts.

I jumped into overdrive then, throwing on a navy blue sweater dress with a thin brown belt around my waist and a pair of kit boots to match. I shoved some silver bangles on my wrist and was working on my hoop earrings as I ran out the door.

Cami answered the front door with her usual smirk that had grown on me last time. I was surprised to see something that looked like happiness in her eyes. I surprised her, in turn, by giving her a big hug.

"Whoa, I'm happy to see you, too," she said, instantly pulling me away from her.

She gave me a "you're weird" look, but I didn't care. Cade was standing in the living room, looking bored until his mom came in, wiping her hands on her apron. She elbowed him and he moved forward to shake Mom's hand.

"Cade is the man of the house tonight," she proudly informed us. "He gets to cut the turkey and everything."

Cami gave her pointer finger a whirl in the air and mouthed, "Woo Hoo." Cade shot her a mean look.

"Isn't your husband here?" Mom asked.

"No, he had to go to Baltimore this week for a conference. Now, with all of the snow, he can't get a flight out."

Now I understood why Cami was so happy. Mom asked Cade to bring in our dishes from the car then followed Mrs. Malone in the kitchen, leaving us alone.

"Can I see your room?" I blurted out.

"Um, sure?" Cami replied, giving me another concerned glance.

I followed her upstairs to the room where Missy and I had shared our first conversation. That seemed like a lifetime ago. Cami plopped down on the middle of her bed and looked at me, but said nothing. I noticed her mom hadn't made a big deal about her jeans and sweatshirt. I sat on the edge of the bed and stared out the window. There was so much I wanted to say but had no idea where to begin.

I guess Cami sensed my distress because finally she said, "So, I take it you have something big to tell me."

I gave her a questioning look.

"You're strung so tight you look like you're about to snap. I take it something is going on between you and my little brother."

I just stared at her dumbly, mouth moving like a guppy, but with nothing coming out. Cami got off her bed and started toward the door.

"Look, I like you and all but I have enough drama in my life without having to deal with my brother's girlfriend. I'm sorry if he screwed you over or something. I thought he really liked you." She looked genuinely confused, but shook it off and opened the door. "I hope you guys work things out. I really do."

She made no move to leave. I realized she was waiting for me to go. I stood up to walk out. I made it to the other side of the bed before something in me kicked on like a light switch. I felt brave. I walked over, moved the door from her hand and closed it instead.

"I know about your father, Cami," I said, looking her straight in the eyes. "I know what he did to you."

Much later, we were sitting in her beanbags under the window. Her back was to me, giving me access to her long, beautiful hair. I had already braided half of it; dozens of golden strands fell across her shoulders. I picked up another handful and began to brush, listening to her talk. Her words came out muffled because of her stuffy nose. The dozens of crumbled up tissues and our swollen faces were the only evidence left of the agony we had just relived. I forced myself to step out of the past and listen to Cami.

"It's so strange to actually tell someone everything," she said.

"You never told anyone?" I asked.

The pain of knowing what she had endured in silence as a child struck me again. I took a deep breath. Cami instinctively reached back and held the half-finished braid so I could grab another tissue. I dabbed my eyes and went back to work on her hair.

After grabbing her own tissue, she continued, "I told my aunt once. Dad's sister. She was always so sweet to me. She found me crying outside at Grandmother's house one day and wouldn't stop bugging me until I told her."

"What happened?" I asked.

By the way Cami started crying again, I dreaded the answer. "I told her the only way I knew how with the very limited vocabulary I had at that age." She drew a ragged breath and continued, "She called me a liar. Actually, she called me a lot worse because of the things I knew."

I didn't know what to say so I just hugged her back to me and held her as she sobbed.

Cami's sobs had diminished to quiet sniffles when we heard a knock on the door. Cade opened it and told us dinner was ready. He must have heard the crying, because he walked in and found us. He looked from Cami's tear-streaked face to mine and back again before exploding.

"What have you done to her?" he yelled at me.

Cami was out of the bag and in front of him in a heartbeat.

"What do you mean, doofus?" she demanded pushing him in the chest. "Ember hasn't done anything but help me. She knew things about me and she actually cared," she added, more calmly.

"Really? She knew things, huh?" he asked with a sneer. "Did she tell you how she knows these things? Did she happen to mention that she thinks God tells her things about people? Did she?" he barked through gritted teeth.

Cami looked back at me as if to question if what her brother saying was true. I could only drop my eyes in response. I help my breath, dreading what was coming next.

"So what?" Cami demanded.

That was not what I expected to hear. I thought she was going to hate me, like Cade did. He looked at me, then her, in disbelief.

"*So what?* She's hears voices, Cami. They tell her things," he added slowly, then he began pacing the room like a caged animal. "And you believe her. That makes you almost as crazy as she is," he huffed, heading for the door.

"Yeah, and you believed that fortune teller at the county fair last year when she said you were going to be rich and famous," Cami taunted.

Cade didn't take the bait. Instead, he just turned to her with grief in his eyes. "That was three years ago, Cami. I was just a kid and believing was just part of the fun. Everyone knew she was a fake, even the woman." He strode over and grabbed Cami by the shoulders. "Ember believes it is real, Cami. That is the difference. I don't know how she found out whatever little secret you had, but it doesn't matter." He let go of Cami, pointed at me and said, "Ember is a liar."

I dropped my head into my hands, unable to stop the tears this time. I hurt so badly; it was hard to breathe. I couldn't look up to see Cami but I could hear her tears as her anger welled up again and spilt over on Cade.

"How dare you! How dare you call her a liar! You said you were in love with her! How do you love someone, but then call them a liar? I know what that feels like, Cade!" she couldn't hold back the tears anymore.

With a sob, she told Cade to get out. I heard the door click shut, then Cami knelt beside me and we wept together, again.

What seemed like hours later, Cami and I went downstairs, hunger driving us out of the room. We had cleaned up, but I still felt very conspicuous as we walked into the living room. Our mothers were chatting on the couch with steaming mugs of coffee. They gave us both reassuring smiles before letting us know they had put a couple of plates aside for us. Cade was nowhere to be seen.

"That was weird," Cami whispered as we walked into the kitchen to claim our food. "Yeah, I can't imagine missing Thanksgiving dinner and getting away with it."

The heaping plates of turkey and dressing grabbed our attention, and any awkwardness disappeared. We took our plates in the living room and sat on the floor to eat, deciding to get in some family time on the holiday. Our mothers were happy to see us and soon all four of us were talking and having a good time. Later, Cami and I went to clean up our dishes. I couldn't help but ask if she planned to do anything now that she had confronted her past. Her hands stilled under the water as she considered it.

"I don't know, maybe nothing," she said, making me glance over at her with a frown. "Don't worry," she said, seeing my reaction. "I think it was good for to me talk about it. All the crying couldn't have hurt, either," she added with a chuckle. "I feel better. Thanks."

It was nice to have someone on my side for once so I didn't argue, though I was disappointed. Secretly, I had hoped that Cami would have decided to start counseling or even asked me about salvation. Just having a good cry didn't really seem like enough. Instead of voicing my concern, I gave her a smile. The moms interrupted before we could say more. Between the four of us, we cleaned the kitchen quickly, then it was time to go. Cami and I exchanged numbers then we all walked out to our car and the conversation started up again. I noticed I didn't have my purse, so I told them I would go in and grab it. I heard Mom call across the yard as I ran in, saying she had put it on the coat rack by the back door.

"Let go," I murmured to the rack as I tried to untangle my purse strap from it.

"Do you need some help?" asked a familiar voice behind me.

I swung around to find Mr. Malone sitting at the little kitchen table, with a plate in front of him.

"I thought you were gone," was all I could manage to say.

"Well, it's nice to see you too," he teased, easing up from his seat to walk over to me. I unconsciously stepped back, still holding onto my entangled purse. "I finally got a flight in. I didn't want to interrupt dinner so I got a cab home. I came in while all of you were busy in the kitchen cleaning up."

He had been there that whole time but didn't even tell anyone. The thought distressed me.

As if knowing what I was thinking, he answered, "I went up to change and visit with Cade for a while. By the time I came down, y'all were outside so I decided to surprise the rest of my family when you leave."

His message was clear. He didn't want my mother and me there. That was OK with me.

"Well, we're leaving now," I said, now frantically pulling at my purse.

He walked over to me, reached up, and freed my purse. I mumbled "thanks" and turned to walk away when I realized he was still holding the strap.

"I'm happy to help, Ember," he said, staring at me. "In fact, I think we can help each other."

My hands started shaking as I waited to hear him out. I didn't have a choice. He let go of my purse and walked away back over to the table. He lifted a paper out of a black binder.

"It looks like I'm not the only one who has a few secrets. I checked you out. It seems like you have a wild streak in you, even had a few run-ins with the law." He looked down at the paper and smiled. "They all got covered up quickly, but I know how to dig up the truth. It would be a shame for this to come out, right when your momma seems to be so happy here."

My whole body was shaking now. I had to get out of there. I turned and ran right into Cade.

"What's going on?" he demanded, no doubt sensing the tension.

"Oh, nothing for you to worry about," his dad said with a smile. "Ember and I are just coming to a little understanding, aren't we, hon?"

I didn't look at either of them as I ran out of the room.

It was dark and cold when I got outside so it was easy to hide my tears and trembles. Mom was more than happy to carry the conversation on the way home so I didn't have to talk. The phone rang as soon as we walked in. Mom answered it and went to talk back in her room, leaving me safe again. I quickly emptied the empty dishes out of the car and jumped into the shower. It took a long time under the steaming water for my body to stop shaking. I put on my pajamas and went straight to bed, praying for sleep. Mom tapped on my door. I steeled myself for questions, but instead, she sat on my bed quietly. I was the one to ask if she was OK. She looked over at me. I could see her sad smile in the dim light from the hall.

"Ember, that was Mrs. Denton on the phone. She didn't want to bother us on Thanksgiving, but she thought you would want to know."

I sat up and stared at Mom. She looked away.

"Honey, Granny passed away tonight."

I fell back onto the bed, pressing the palms of my hands against my head to try to stop the tears. I was so tired of crying.

"No, please no," I begged, then started to sob.

Mom was clearly surprised at my reaction.

"Ember, listen to me," she said, taking my hand. "I know you two had something special between you, but this is too much." She stood up and began pacing the room. "Look at me," she demanded softly. "You cannot break down because of this. That woman was well over 100 years old, Ember. She had lived a very full life. She was even able to say goodbye to almost all of her relatives today. They were all there for Thanksgiving." I didn't respond, so she continued, "You of all people should know that she was a good, Christian woman. She's in heaven now."

I just rolled over into a fetal position, which seemed to exasperate Mom. She threw her hands up and stared at me awhile. I didn't blame her. I had been an emotional wreck for weeks. Everyone had a limit.

"Granny's funeral will be Sunday. I'll be in my room if you want to talk," she said, then left my room, quietly closing the door behind her.

Chapter Nine

"**I**T'S TIME TO get up," Mom ordered, opening my curtains. I peeked out from under my pillow at the blinding light, then quickly went back for cover.

"I'm still on break," I reminded her.

"Yes, and it's the day after Thanksgiving. We've never missed one Black Friday sale and I don't intend to start now. Let's go."

She turned to my closet to pick out something for me to wear while I worked to sit up. She knew I wouldn't argue with her about clothes today.

"We are going to drive up to Atlanta and do some real shopping." She turned back to look at me. Her voice wavered, "How... how does that sound?"

I just nodded and took the clothes from her hands on my way to the bathroom. I thought I had seen tears in her eyes.

The threat of her tears was enough to make me bite back a retort. "Sounds great!" I responded with enthusiasm I didn't feel.

We were on our way fifteen minutes later.

She might not have understood everything that was going on with me, but Mom was good at knowing what could bring me out of a funk. She had done it a lot through the years, especially as a low-income single parent. That day was no different. She let me drive my car, though it meant she got to choose the songs.

We had a drive-thru biscuit breakfast, and a complete 90's play-list to sing our way through. By the time we got to the mall, my spirits were already lighter. It was nice to get out of my head for a while.

We didn't make it in time for the Early Bird specials, but there were still plenty of great sales. Mom pulled out her Christmas list and we started shopping for friends and family. By the time lunch rolled around, we were tired and hungry.

"I thought that mega-biscuit would have lasted longer," she teased as we strolled through the food court, trying to choose where to eat.

Mom's phone rang so we stopped as she balanced shopping bags on an empty table while trying to find it. I reached over and took it from her back pocket.

"You wanted it close, remember?" She grabbed it from me with a smirk and checked the number.

"It's Gloria from work," she informed me.

I stood there waiting, feeling a little like a pack donkey. She asked her friend to hold on a second and turned to me, "Why don't you pick us something and bring it back here. You can leave the bags," she added.

The temptation to be free of the bags won over having to order alone. She pressed some money into my hand and I went in search of lunch.

I decided to have Chick-Fil-A and made a dash for it, knocking into someone in my anxiousness to eat.

"Sorry," I muttered and continued on my way until someone grabbed my arm. I guess I was still jumpy from the night before, because I yanked it away and turned to the person. I couldn't believe my eyes. Out of the entire city of Atlanta, I had run into my old friend, Tara. Truly, things could not get worse. Hold that thought; two more of them stepped out from behind her, standing staggered, in perfect cheerleader form. They stood there grinning at me with over-polished teeth; only pompoms were needed to complete the little ensemble. They squealed and bounced around me until I was dizzy.

"Tell us everything," one demanded as we sat at the nearest empty booth.

I began telling them, in as little detail as possible, what had been going on with me since I left Atlanta. They were beginning to look a little bored until one screeched, "Boys!" They all became animated again, wanting to know about the guys I had met. I told them about a few that I had met on the beach over spring break.

"But what about where you live?" Tara asked. "And who are you with? The quarterback, I hope," she added and the others giggled.

I cringed at the thought of Reid and the dance, which caused more questions. We all continued to talk and laugh about nothing of importance, which was a nice change for me. It was easy to just slip back into my old life again and forget about my problems. Finally, I told them a little about Cade, and our break-up, telling them we just didn't see things the same way.

"It sounds like you've got quite a lot of drama going on in that little town of yours," Tara said, barely containing her glee.

"You don't know the half of it," I said, rolling my eyes.

"But maybe we should," Sarah added mysteriously.

"You are so brilliant!" agreed Amber, though I wasn't exactly sure what they were agreeing to, until Tara exclaimed, "Road trip!"

After a lot of excited planning, we finally said our goodbyes with the promise to set up a date for them to come visit soon.

When I got back to Mom, she was just hanging up the phone, not even realizing how long I was gone. We ate and completed our shopping list, not making it home until dark. Exhausted, we both said goodnight and went straight to our rooms. I tried to pray, but I couldn't seem to get into it, so I gave up and went to sleep.

The next day, we followed tradition by putting up our Christmas tree. It was a little strange, just Mom and me, but we played all of our old favorite Christmas songs, made cider, and made the best of it. The six-foot, dollar store tree was miniature compared to what we had used the last few years, so it didn't take long to decorate. After lunch, we decided to take advantage of the extra time and wrap presents. By bedtime, we had all of the gifts wrapped and stored in the office closet, all ready for our Christmas trip to Florida.

It was Sunday before I was ready. I had pushed the funeral to the back of my mind, but there was no ignoring it today. I was wearing a simple, black long-sleeved dress and pumps when Mom found me staring out the kitchen window. She stood beside me and gave me a gentle squeeze.

"Are you certain you don't need me to come with you? I can bow out of Gloria's baby shower this afternoon," she offered.

We had already been over it that morning when I first got up. I knew I could do this alone.

"I'm sure," I said giving her a reassuring smile.

"You are a special person. You know that, right?" she asked.

I kissed her cheek then my cell rang. It was Camille.

"Hi, Cami," I said as I walked back to my room. I sat on my bed as she asked, "You sound upset. Am I interrupting anything?"

"I was just on the way out the door, but I'm a little early. How are you? Do you need something?"

"Actually, I feel better than I have in, well, as long as I can remember. And no, I don't need anything. I just wanted you to be the first to know, since I never would have been able to do this without you."

"What do you mean?"

"Well, Dad showed up Thursday after you left. So, of course, I made a quick getaway. The next day, I bumped into a friend who is also a, you know, an abuse counselor. I was able to really talk to her about everything, without sobbing the whole time, which helped it go a lot faster." She laughed. "Anyway, I've decided I'm going to tell Mom and maybe after that, I don't know for sure, but I'm thinking I may go ahead and, you know, press charges and everything against my dad."

I let out a gush of breath I didn't realize I was holding and fell back on my bed. This is what I had hoped for Cami, until her dad threatened me. If she went ahead with this, he would know I had a part in it.

"Hey, are you there?" Cami asked, interrupting my dark thoughts.

I couldn't discourage her, even though it meant certain pain for me. I closed my eyes and ignored my fear.

"That's amazing, Cami. I'm so happy for you."

"Really? You had me worried there for a minute. You were so quiet."

"I'm sorry. It's just a lot to take in and I'm worried about everything."

"Don't worry about me. Mom needs to know what she's married to and I need to do this so I can get on with my life. I'm tired of running. Ember, can I ask you for a favor?" Cami added quietly.

"Anything," I said without hesitation.

"Would you pray for me? I mean, not now, but over the next few days when things get tough."

"Yeah, of course I will." After we hung up, I didn't have time to think about anything. I would be late for the funeral.

The small country church was almost full by the time I arrived. I decided not to take one of the few remaining seats away from family, so I stood in the entryway instead. There were others with me. In fact, people spilled outdoors and around the sides of the church. They left the windows cracked, in spite of the cold, so everyone could hear the service. It was long. Person after person took their turn standing up and saying nice things about Granny. The singing went on and on. My legs ached by the time it was over, but it was worth it. It was a beautiful service and tribute to Granny. At the last moment, I decided to join the procession to the cemetery. I didn't feel like I had really been able to say goodbye to her yet. I stood in the back again, not going forward to say goodbye to Granny until the last of the family had paid their respects. There were only a few people left when I stepped up to the coffin. A single tear fell down my face as I laid a flower on top of it. I looked up to find Mrs. Denton standing close by. I walked over to her and she gave me one of her trademark bear hugs.

"I'm so sorry," I whispered.

She took my hand and led me to one of the family's chairs. I just stared at the ground, willing my tears to stop.

"I wasn't ready for her to go," I said with a catch in my throat. "I know it sounds selfish, but I still need her."

To my surprise, Mrs. Denton let out a laugh. Obviously, she was lost in her grief.

She patted my hand. "Honey, she only stuck around as long

as she did because of you. She wouldn't have left if you still needed her," she added with a smile.

"No offense, Mrs. Denton, but that's the craziest thing I have ever heard," I admitted.

"No it's not. The doctors have been saying she was going to pass over for years. She gave us quite a scare last year around this time; she even went into a coma for a few days. When she came out of that, she told me there was someone she needed to stay on this Earth for. The feisty thing prayed for more time and fought that sickness for months. She got better right before you showed up this summer."

I didn't know what to say. It certainly sounded like Granny. The thought of her fighting back death made me smile.

"She left something for you. I found it in her Bible yesterday," Mrs. Denton said as she passed me an unopened envelop with my name on it.

Tears dripped down my face. I didn't try to stop them this time.

"Do you mind giving me a minute to read it first, before I show it to you?" I asked, knowing she would want to know what her grandmother had written in her last days.

"I can do better than that," she said, standing. "I have to go feed all of these hungry folks. You read that letter when you're ready." I thanked her and looked back at the letter. "What Granny wrote to you in that letter, it's between you and her. I don't want to know, unless you need to talk about it, understand?" she asked.

I wiped my face and nodded again. She gave me another hug.

"That was from Violet. She wanted so much to be here."

Mrs. Denton let out a sigh and walked over to the coffin. I watched as she placed a hand on it, then she walked away. When she was gone, I did the same, holding the unopened letter close to my heart. I didn't want to open it. I knew it wasn't sensible, but I couldn't help but feel that once I read her words, she would really be gone.

Mom must have been still at her friend's shower because the house was empty when I got home. I turned my phone back on to see if there was a message from her, but only Tara had texted. She and her friends wanted me to meet them halfway at a new dance club next weekend. The next text read, *Bring Cade!*

I kicked off my heels, walked to the living room, and slumped on the couch, letting the grief wash over me. I was so tired of all this hurt and pain. It would be so easy to just drop all of this and be a normal teenager again, to get involved with Cade and have fun with my old friends. It sounded so appealing right then. I couldn't remember why I was so upset with him. I sent him a text, thinking he probably wouldn't answer, but he did. Cade asked me to come over, saying his parents were home. I didn't know what to say. I looked over and saw Granny's letter lying on the couch beside me. I picked it up and gently tore open the envelope, excited to hear her wisdom again. I opened the folded letter and stared at the paper in disbelief. There were only six words scribbled across the page.

It read, "They can't hurt a dead man."

Poor Granny, I thought, *she must have been in a little out of it toward the end.*

I sent Cade a text. I told him I would be over soon. I felt sick after I sent it. I really didn't want to go back, but I couldn't keep going like I was. I leaned over with a groan, cupping my face in my hands.

Please help me, I cried out to God.

I tried to pray, but was so tired I couldn't. I had no idea what to say. I remembered what Kyle had told me that night at the revival. I knelt by the couch and started to pray, in a heavenly language.

An hour later, I was standing at Cade's door. He seemed genuinely happy to see me as he pulled me into a hug. I told him about my friends' plans the next weekend. Cade was immediately excited about the idea of meeting them. I felt a twinge of hurt. Only a few weeks ago, I had sat in this room with him, crying about how they had treated me. I was tired of being different, though. I wanted my old life back, so I pushed the thought away. We spent the next hour on the phone with Tara, making introductions and working out details. After we hung up, I told Cade how glad I was that we were together again. I think I hoped that speaking the words aloud would dispel the doubt I felt.

"I knew you would come around. So do you want to go upstairs to play some video games and catch up on old times?" he asked with a wink. "Wait! Let me go clean up the room a little first. I'll be right back down," Cade said, bounding up the stairs before I could answer.

"Well, look who's back," said Mr. Malone as he walked in from his office, startling me. "I heard my daughter is coming home next weekend to have a talk with her mother. You wouldn't know anything about that, would you, Ember? Or do I need to be a good neighbor and let the parents around here know exactly what kind of girl is hanging around their children?"

This could not be happening. I stumbled back, trying to look for Cade. Mr. Malone was still waiting for an answer, but I couldn't put together a coherent thought.

Then, six words came to my mind so I said them, "You can't hurt a dead man," and then I smiled.

"You *are* crazy."

"No, I'm not—and it turns out, neither was Granny," I said with a laugh, no longer afraid. "The Word says, 'If Christ is in you, though the body is dead because of sin, the spirit is alive because of righteousness.' Yes, I sinned and I suffered because of it, but I am dead to that. I am a new creature in Christ. Do you hear me, Mr. Malone? That person is dead, so go ahead and tell anyone you want to about my past. I don't care. I will stand by your daughter as long as she wants me there. You will not scare me into backing down."

I looked up to see Cade at the bottom of the stairs, looking confused as he stared at the two of us.

"I believe her," I added quietly as I heard Mr. Malone storm out, his office door slamming behind him. I didn't turn away from Cade, though. "I'm sorry, Cade. I thought I could go back, but I can't. I don't want to. I would still like to be friends, though. If you can accept me like I am."

He sat on the bottom stair, staring out across the living room, not looking at me. I walked over and sat by him.

"And, I forgive you."

"I didn't ask you to," he muttered under his breath.

"I know you didn't, but I don't think I have ever been hurt so badly by anyone, Cade. Your sister was right. When you didn't believe me, that was the worst kind of betrayal. Please remember that when Cami comes home next weekend."

He didn't answer so I stood up and walked to the door. With a sigh, I continued, "That's why I choose to forgive you. There's no way I'm going to walk around with that kind of hurt. It's debilitating. I really am sorry things didn't work out."

I was almost out the door when I heard him whisper, "me too," but I didn't go back. For the first time in weeks, I felt like a weight had been lifted off me. Things weren't perfect, but at least I knew where I stood.

Monday, I was back in school. My circumstances hadn't changed, but my outlook was better. Maybe some of the kids sensed it, because they seemed friendlier toward me that week— but then again, maybe it was just my attitude. The big surprise came Friday afternoon. Missy texted me and asked if I would meet her at the drive-in restaurant in town. I was in the middle of working on my homework, but curiosity got the best of me. I told her I could be there right away.

The after-school crowd had thinned out, leaving only a couple of other cars. I parked away from them in case Missy wanted to talk privately. A couple of minutes later, Missy rode up on her bike. She parked it in front of my car and opened the door.

"Is this OK?" she asked. "My car is in the shop."

I told her it was so she hopped in next to me. We decided to order shakes and passed the time talking about the youth group and school until they were brought out to us. After the waitress skated back to the restaurant, Missy apologized.

"I know I have been distant lately. No, that's not right. Actually I haven't been a friend to you at all and I'm sorry."

I had a hundred questions running through my brain, but I had learned from experience not to overwhelm her. Instead, I said thanks and sipped on my milkshake, hoping she would say more. She did.

"You and Cade were fighting and well, I hated being in the middle. But Cade and I have been friends since forever, and..."

"And you had to choose a side so of course the oldest friend gets the support." I finished for her. "I understand." I did understand, but I didn't like it. Sometimes it bites, being the new kid. "It's not that simple, Ember. It's not just that I've known

Cade longer," she said, wrapping a napkin around her milk-shake. "He's always stuck up for me. Kids can be cruel and I was, well, mousy. You wouldn't believe how many fights he got in because of me. He's been like a protective big brother and I've never been able to repay him, until now. I didn't agree with him, though."

I looked at her, surprised.

"I didn't, and I told him so but he wouldn't budge even though he was hurting." Missy took a drink of her milkshake, then continued, "Cade showed up at the back to school party that night. Did you know?"

I hadn't known and told her so.

"That's why I left early," Missy said. I waited for her to elaborate, but instead she said, "I believe he was really in love with you."

It was very hard to hear. All of it was just tearing open old wounds. "Why are you telling me this now?" I snapped, harder than I intended. I was unable to mask the irritation and hurt.

Missy swallowed, but bravely continued, "Cade called me a few nights ago and told me it was over between the two of you." She looked at me as if to gauge my reaction. I focused on my shake. "He said he was ready to move on. I didn't really believe him and kind of stayed on standby just in case until today." She gave me another nervous glance. "He told me he was in love…"

I didn't know whether to laugh or cry.

"…with one of your old friends. Cade called her right after you walked out that night and they met halfway at some club. He left right after school today to go Atlanta for the weekend."

My decision was made. I had to laugh at the irony of it. Missy must have mistaken it for happiness because she sounded relieved. "Well, I'm happy, really happy that it's over—the fighting, I mean. I even told Cade that I was never going to be caught in the middle like that again. For anyone." She tossed her empty cup in the bag then turned to look at me. "I know you have every right to hate me, but I really hope we can be friends again."

"Missy," I began, "It was hard not having you around through all of this and I'll admit, it would have been nice to understand why you were so distant. I just assumed it was because you thought I was crazy. But, I always considered you my friend, through all of it. I still do." Missy gave me a big smile and hug, then I went on. "I thought I scared you, like I did Cade."

"Yeah, a little," she admitted shyly. "But, I saw Noah at the back to school party and we started talking. He invited me to his church, so I went with him and Ella."

I almost choked. "Seriously? What did you think?"

"Well, I didn't have a big God experience, not like you. He told me a little about that, by the way. I hope you don't mind."

"No, of course not. So, are you going to go back?"

"I think I would like to know a little more about what they believe, about the gifts of the Spirit first. In fact, it's probably not so great of me to ask a favor after I just apologized, but..."

I just rolled my eyes as I slurped up the last of my shake.

"Do you think we might be able to get together again sometime so you could tell me more about your experience? I mean, it's great talking to Noah, but I think it would be helpful coming from someone who hasn't been raised with it their whole life."

"Sure, but I haven't even been able to wrap my head around everything yet; so much has happened."

"It doesn't have to be right away. Maybe it would help if you took some notes, like a journal."

"That's a good idea. Maybe we can get together after Christmas break."

"Great, thanks," said Missy with a smile. "Let's not wait that long to just hang out, though, OK?"

"Definitely. I've got to get home for dinner now."

"OK, I'll see you in the morning for our trip to the Samaritan's Purse warehouse and we'll make some plans. And don't forget about the Winter Ball," she said, getting out of the car.

"I had forgotten about it." I let down the window and asked, "You want to go together?"

"Well, I was thinking about asking Noah, but you could come with us," she offered through the window.

"Not a chance I'm crashing your date to the ball!" I said in mock horror, "but I'll be your standby."

We said our goodbyes and I left for home. After dinner, I took Missy's advice and began writing down some of the things that had happened to me over the past few months. It was a slow process, and my thoughts kept me up well into the night.

We met early the next morning for the drive to Atlanta. There were teens from youth groups all over town volunteering, so we took the big bus. By the time I reached the church, it was about to pull out, thanks to my late night. I dashed up the steps and found that, thankfully, Missy had saved me a seat. She even let me sit by the window. I asked her if she had asked Noah to the dance. Missy informed me that he was on the bus and that she would ask him later.

"He's here?" I asked, propping myself up to look around. I spotted him a few rows back. "Go talk to him," I commanded, "You'll chicken out if you don't."

"Ember, I already let Cade come between us." I rolled my eyes and gave her a little nudge with my shoulder. She laughed and held on to the seat. "Someone is probably sitting with him anyway," she insisted.

I had to admit, it was a possibility. It was too crowded to be sure. "Maybe, but it would only take a minute to check. Just act like you're going to the bathroom."

Missy didn't budge.

"Well, you're going to have a boring time with me," I said, yawning, "I'm going to sleep."

I leaned against the window and closed my eyes. After a few minutes, I heard Missy grumble and move out of the seat, making me smile. I stayed where I was, though. I really was sleepy. Only a few minutes passed before she was back.

"Oh no. Bad news?" I asked, but it wasn't Missy. It was too early to deal with this. *You can't hurt a dead man,* I repeated in my head, then said with dread, "Hi, Reid." He didn't return my greeting. I sat up and turned sideways to face my fear. I expected him to be exuding angry vibes, but he just looked uncomfortable. He rubbed his hands on the knees of his jeans and looked everywhere but at me. Did I freak everyone out? I just wanted it to be over.

As if answering my silent thought he said, "I don't know how to start."

"Just say it please, Reid," I asked in defeat, turning to rest my head on the window again.

"I'm sorry," he whispered.

I sat up and asked him if I heard him right.

"Yeah, I'm sorry for yelling at you that night after the party and for how I've acted since then. When you said that about me in front of my friends...it was really tough for me," he admitted.

I cringed. I had spent most of the time feeling sorry for myself because of the way I was being treated. I realized now, I had never taken the time to see it from his point of view. "Reid, I am so sorry," I said truthfully, "I should have apologized a long time ago. I had no right to blurt it out like that in front of everyone."

He kept his head down, but I saw him nod.

"I shouldn't have said it, but I was so worried about you. The thought of you cutting yourself..." I looked away, wishing I could hide from the truth.

He looked around nervously, obviously concerned someone might have heard me. Between the roar of the bus and the even louder teens, it wasn't a possibility.

Once he knew it was safe he answered with a sigh, "A couple of those were my teammates. As quarterback, I'm kind of the leader of the group. If the whole team found out I was having such a hard time with emotional stuff. If they thought there was a real possibility that I might get benched..." He trailed off, leaving his real worry hidden.

"But, the season is over. Is that why you're talking to me about this now?"

"I'm apologizing now because I talked to Pastor Eric about it. Someone told him that I was angry with you and he wanted to know what was going on. Since then, he's been helping me sort things out and praying with me. And, I was sitting by Noah when Missy walked by, so I asked her to switch seats with me."

Well, at least Missy was having a nice time, I thought glumly. I still felt terrible that Reid put so much pressure on himself to play ball, and told him so.

"It's not just me," he said with a humorless laugh. "My dad has always expected me to play football in college, like he used to. He gave me a hard time when he found out. He said no 'respectable Christian' would do the sort of thing I was doing to myself. I was really messed up, especially because my mom died around that time."

Once again, I felt horrible, but didn't interrupt again.

"Anyway, Pastor Eric encouraged me to talk to Coach. I did, after the last game, and it turns out he was really great about it."

I started to apologize again but he stopped me.

"No, it was hard but if you hadn't said anything, well, I know I wouldn't have spoken up. Coach was upset that I kept it to myself for so long," Reid bounced his knee nervously as he continued. "He wanted me to see him as a friend I could talk to, not just a coach. Anyway, he found me a shrink. I'm thinking about going. So, in a way, I should be thanking you. You still look upset. Don't you believe me?" he asked, watching me intently now.

"It's just hard to forget how mad you were," I confessed, thinking about that night.

"That's not the only reason I was upset," he began. He looked away from me, seeming on edge again.

"OK everyone, we've almost arrived at the warehouse. I need your attention for a minute," interrupted Pastor Eric and the moment was gone.

We all were herded off the bus and into groups. I was with Ella and Kyle. I enjoyed talking to them again. We were given a short introduction into the program then escorted into the warehouse to begin sorting. I only saw Missy once across the room. She mouthed, "Are you OK?" I gave her a big smile to reassure her, though I was still feeling uneasy about the unfinished conversation.

A few hours later, our time was up so we all shuffled back to the bus, feeling tired but fulfilled. Everyone was already talking about going back to volunteer the next year.

I pulled Missy aside quickly while everyone was lining up. "How did it go?" I asked quickly.

Noah walked up at that time so I didn't get any details about the ball, but the silly grin on both of their faces said enough.

"I guess you guys will sit together," Noah asked, with resignation.

"If it's OK with Ember, I would like to finish our talk," Reid said from behind me, surprising me. Everyone seemed happy with that, so Reid and I made our way onto the bus together.

I was a nervous wreck by the time the bus left the parking lot. Obviously, I wasn't the only one.

"It's never been this difficult to talk to a girl," he mumbled to himself.

I watched his hand disappear in his dark hair as he mussed it up anxiously. "You were saying that you were mad at me for some reason, other than opening my big mouth."

That seemed to get him focused again. He said with a smile, "Yeah. Well, the thing is, I had thought you and Malone were together."

My stomach tightened at the reference to Cade, but I listened silently as he went on.

"I mentioned something about it earlier when I saw him at the dance and he told me absolutely not, like it was a crazy idea."

I must have made some kind of noise because Reid glanced at me, but I gave him a weak smile.

"Anyway, I was hoping I would get a chance to talk to you and I finally did when we were putting up the tables that night. Before I could say anything, though, you made that Superman comment," he laughed at my expression, "yeah, I still remember that. Then, you ran over to the others, and it didn't go so great from there."

"Yeah, I know," I muttered.

"I wanted to ask you to the Winter Ball," he blurted.

"Me?" I squeaked. "I had no idea you would...that you...," I stuttered, unsure how to finish.

"You remember the time we hung out at the youth conference?" he asked. "I really liked you then...well, probably before that."

I tried to remember when we had spoken before.

"You blew me away the first time I saw you. I was throwing the football in front of the church that first night you visited."

My stomach was doing somersaults now. I grinned down at my hands and was about to say thanks. Instead, I thought of Cade. I didn't want to ruin this before it started, but I wasn't going to repeat that again if I could help it. I looked up at him again hesitantly.

"That's really sweet, but I need to tell you something. Remember those teens from another church who were on our team that night we met?"

"Yeah, I warned you not to go to their church."

"Well, I went. They don't handle snakes, like you were worried about, but they do believe in the gifts of the Spirit—and so do I, Reid. That's how I knew about you...your problem," I stammered nervously. "I have the gift of knowledge." It was the first time I had spoken it aloud. It sounded strange, even to my own ears.

"OK," he said, simply.

"OK?" I asked, taken aback. "You were freaking about them!"

He shrugged nonchalantly. "So, I'm scared of snakes. Great, now you know my other weakness," he said with an exaggerated sigh, "and I don't know any of yours."

"That would be a very long conversation for another day. I

can't believe you don't think I'm weird because I know things sometimes."

"He's God, Ember. I'm not. I'm not going to put Him in a box. So, will you go with me to the ball?"

I just stared at him, amazed at his simple faith. He obviously mistook it for indecision.

"We could go with a group, if you'd rather."

"Yeah, I'd love to."

We stopped for some dinner in the food court of a mall. Noah, Missy, Ella, Kyle and a couple of Reid's friends sat with us. Before we were done, the news of our dates was out and we all decided to go as a group. We had fun planning the details, from what to drive to coordinating clothes. Thankfully, the matching clothes idea was cut right away. By the time I got home that evening, I was exhausted but happier than I had been in a long time.

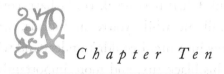

Chapter Ten

I T WAS QUITE a challenge to close the door of the limousine
while pushing back yards of taffeta and satin. When Reid
finally succeeded, he leaned back on the white car with a
sigh. He offered his arm to me with a smile. My gown, a full
length, black velvet strapless dress with a satin wrap, had its
own voluminous skirt to control. I gladly reached for his arm as
the other couples in our group let down the windows and leaned
out, tormenting us with obnoxious whistles and yells.

"Maybe I should have put a little more consideration in the
whole group date thing," Reid lamented, throwing a black look
back toward the limo.

The catcalls abruptly stopped, though, with the sound of a
yelp; someone must have gotten caught in the window as it was
quickly let up. Soft light spilled over us as we stopped on my
front porch. The cold air made my words come out in a puff of
cold air.

"I had a wonderful time tonight," I told him. It was the truth.
We had danced almost every dance and spent the rest of the
time laughing and hanging around our friends. The thought of
actually having such a diverse group of friends was exhilarating
in itself. He reached up and straightened my crown. I still found
it hard to believe we were crowned the king and queen of the

ball. The memory made me smile. I watched as Reid weaved his fingers through mine. When I looked up, he was watching me.

"I don't think Christmas break could have come at a worse time. You'll call me while you're in Florida, won't you?" he asked, somehow insecure. I couldn't understand why. He was so handsome in his black tux, and more importantly, his love for Christ was apparent. It was an anomaly, but Reid's gentleness and humility made him strong.

He tenderly reached up and moved a curl from my cheek as he waited for me to respond. My breath caught and I could only nod as I looked up into his ice-blue eyes. I wasn't cold any longer. He hesitated for another moment then dropped his hand from my face. Backing up a step, our hands fell apart, leaving me cold again as the moment ended. I couldn't help but feel a twinge of disappointment, but only for a moment. I didn't want to rush this. From the look of determination on his face, Reid felt the same way. He walked away, but stopped at the limo.

"I'm looking forward to hanging out with you when you get back!" he called across the yard. He gave me a last smile as he opened the car door. Screams of protest pierced the night as those inside were struck with the cold air and Reid was pulled in the car. The door slammed behind him, abruptly halting their noise, but leaving my laughter in its place. I waved blindly to the tinted windows as they drove away. In spite of the cold, I wasn't ready to go inside and bring an end to the amazing evening. I stood there for a minute longer, hearing only a dog barking in the distance. I reveled in the silence, reciting from memory each smile and laugh that I shared. In the past, I had participated in what I thought was fun, but the old type of partying had always come with pain or regret. Tonight, I only felt pure joy. It felt like a new beginning.

My thoughts were interrupted as a blaring horn cut through the silence of the night. I looked up, surprised to see our limousine making another trip by my house. Standing up through the sunroof was Reid, holding his crown and grinning at me.

"I prayed I would get a chance to see you one more time tonight and you're still there!" he yelled as he was paraded down the street.

I hugged myself against the cold and laughed. I glanced up to the cloudless winter sky, full of stars. My own clouds floated heavenward as I sent up a prayer of thanks.

All of the extended family converged on my grandparents' beach house for a beach-themed Christmas. My creative grandmother decorated their Christmas tree with sand dollars and starfish. The azure-blue ribbons she used as garland were the same color as Reid's eyes. I couldn't help but think about him each time I walked by or lay under the tree with my cousins, as tradition dictated. It was a busy time of baking, carols, wrapping gifts, and enjoying family. In spite of the Christmas bustle, Reid and I still found time to talk on the phone. We didn't talk much about the cutting. He promised that one day he would be ready to share with me. I told Reid I would be happy to listen when he was ready. I knew he was getting help, so I wasn't going to pressure him to talk about it. Besides, there was more to Reid than his scars.

The whole celebration held more meaning for me this year. I found myself in tears during our annual reading of the story of Jesus' birth. My grandparents noticed the difference in me and pulled me aside to hear the story of my rededication. My cousin, Priscilla, whom I'd spent most of the summer with that year, noticed sooner than anyone else. She had personal knowledge of my previous character, considering I took her along to most of the parties. It hurt me to think that I considered myself to be looking out for her that summer. I had been so deceived. My one consolation: I got to witness to Cilla. To my knowledge, she didn't make a decision for Christ, but I know she had to be impacted by the change in me. I mentally added her to my prayer list.

Mom and I left the afternoon after Christmas, sad to leave, but anxious to get back to our home and friends. On the drive back, we talked about just how wonderful that feeling was, to truly belong somewhere. I had texted Missy to let her know I was on the way back. We set up a time to meet on the next afternoon.

I spent the next morning in the office, typing out the handwritten notes I had been taking since the evening we talked at the drive-in. I tried to be as honest as possible, only leaving out my recurring dream. I wanted to share it, but I wasn't sure it was even relevant and I didn't want to scare her. I had just hit "save" and sat back to look over what I had typed when Mom stopped by and told me Missy was there to see me. We made some popcorn and went back to the office to have our talk. Missy, as always, was a wonderful listener, only stopping me occasionally to ask a question. A couple of hours later, I was done with my story. She told me thanks and gave me a big hug as I walked her to the front door. Reid was standing there with a bouquet of flowers, about to knock when I opened it. The three of us chatted on the front porch for a while then decided on a double date, if Noah could go, that Thursday. After the two of them left, the exhaustion from Christmas and from sharing my testimony kicked in. I fell across my bed and didn't wake up until the next morning.

I woke up early, feeling uncomfortable because I had slept in my jeans. I plodded across the hall to brush my teeth and take a hot shower. I was drying my hair when I realized I'd had the dream again. My hair wasn't yet dry, but I turned off the dryer anyway and walked into my room. I sat on the edge of my bed and closed my eyes, waiting in silence, waiting to recall the dream. It was odd, trying to remember. Usually, I struggled to forget. First, I thought I didn't remember immediately because I had been so tired the night before. Then, I abandoned that idea. The dream I had last night was different. Instinctively, I knew I wouldn't be haunted by my recurring dream again. This one was to be my last. With that thought, I pulled my legs up on the bed and concentrated harder.

It all came flooding back then, almost in fast motion; my room, the book, the crashing walls; it was all the same, at first. But then, it slowed down again as I grabbed the sword and walked out into darkness. Unable to help it, my heartbeat quickened and cold sweat dampened my palms. The light from my sword was brighter now, out in the darkness. The cries seemed louder and a chill went down my back as I felt evil near me. I held out my shaking sword, eyes large, as I circled trying to reconcile my fear and a nonexistent assailant. Tears fell freely down my face. I was unwilling to take a hand off my sword to wipe them away. I was scared and so alone. How could I do this by myself? I couldn't answer the fearful question that was gnawing at my insides, terrifying me. I pushed it down and took another step away from my old room and its delusion of safety.

Slowly, I made my way further into the darkness until I was standing in a clearing of a valley. There was nowhere to hide now. I felt completely exposed holding my sword as it burned more intensely, like a white flame. Snarls came from the trees that surrounded the field. The sounds circled me and left me with no way of escape. I closed my eyes and waited for the snarling creatures, my emotions a mixture of both dread and determination. I could hear their heavy footsteps approach, closer and closer. I lifted my eyes to the hills. In the distance, I saw twinkling lights, like stars, as they rushed toward me. Just before the creatures attacked, I realized I was not seeing stars but flaming swords.

I was not alone.

Thursday night, Noah, Reid, and Missy came by to pick me up for the movie. I invited them in while I searched for my jacket in the hall closet. Missy must have mentioned that she and I had talked about what happened to me, because by the time I turned around, holding my jacket triumphantly, they were all looking at me, eyes shining in curiosity. "What?" I asked, still clueless. We didn't make it to the movies that night. Instead, I told my story again. It would become a common occurrence for me over the next few weeks.

As winter turned to spring, more and more teens from Noah's and our youth groups wanted to hear my testimony. They came to my house on Thursday nights and hung out in my living room as I told them about why I rededicated my life to Christ after four years of living a life of a wealthy, party girl. I also told them, in spite of the chance of being ridiculed, about the gift of knowledge I had received. Soon, there was an average of a dozen teens camped out in my living room on Thursday nights. Everyone took turns sharing his or her testimony. We also read the scriptures that affected us that week, prayed for each other, and just listened. Sometimes we just ate and played. I found myself looking forward to those evenings.

One afternoon, Reid dropped me off after school. I was still smiling about one of his jokes when I walked in the living room. Finding Pastor Eric sitting with Mom on my couch was the last thing I had expected. My expression went from happy to confused quickly, sending the two of them scrambling to explain.

Mom was the first one to blurt, "It's not what you think!"

Although shocked, I had enough wits about me to realize it didn't really matter what I thought. Mom was an adult. I was surprised that Pastor Eric would be alone with her because he always had another female around when we talked. I plopped down in the armchair in front of the spindled wall and tried to exude indifference. I was about to tell them how I felt, when Gloria walked in with her new baby. I jumped up and gushed at the adorable bundle. Mom and Pastor Eric were forgotten. Mom explained that Gloria was Pastor Eric's little sister. She wasn't supposed to drive yet, after her C-section, but wanted to get out for a while, so he drove her over. Mom invited the two of them to stay for dinner. I volunteered to hold baby Sam while they got dinner started. Pastor Eric started to follow them to the kitchen, but stopped and came back to sit by me. I hardly noticed. Sam was cute, but Pastor Eric got my attention by clearing his throat.

"I've heard you have a little youth group of your own going on here," he said.

"I wouldn't call it a youth group exactly," I said, cooing at Sam, "some of us get together on Thursday nights just to hang out and pray and stuff but it's not organized or anything." I looked at him again, wondering if he thought it was a bad idea. I remembered how controlling he said the church board could be at times. "Do you have a problem with that?" I asked, probably a little too sharply.

"No, of course not," he assured me. "I'm hearing good things.

Truthfully, I would like to hear your testimony myself sometime." He smiled down at his nephew before continuing. "I guess I need to be honest, though. I do worry a little bit about you guys not having a pastor around to help guide things."

"Are you offering your services?" I asked.

He grinned at me in return. "If you're sure you wouldn't mind an old guy hanging around with the group."

"Nah, of course not. As long as you bring the chips next week."

It had been three weeks since Pastor Eric started coming to our meetings. It was his turn to share his testimony that night. We were all looking forward to it. Before everyone arrived, I decided to spend a few minutes in prayer. I had been sitting on the floor by my bed. When I looked up, my memory wall caught my attention. I crawled over so my memories would be within reach. I lovingly turned over each item in my hands as I thought back. The first item I picked up was Cade's pendant he'd left me on the first day we met. A combination of affection and sadness washed over me as I considered giving it back to him. In the end, I put it back, vowing to use it to remind me to pray for him.

In the next cubby sat my letter from Granny. I reread it with tears in my eyes. Then, I moved down the row reminiscing. There was my crown from the Winter Ball, the strip of blue cloth from the youth conference where I first spoke with Reid, and the seashell Priscilla and I found the day my life was turned upside down. I smiled at the thought of Cilla and felt tears threatening to fall. She had called me a few weeks earlier to tell me she gave her life to Christ.

She wasn't the only new Christian in my family. I reached up to the top left cubby and pulled down a small, wooden cross. Pastor Eric had given it to Mom that night, but she asked me to keep it safe for her. I think Mom gave it to me because she knew how much that memory meant to me. I thought everyone had gone home from the meeting. When I walked into our living room, it was like déjà vu when I saw Pastor Eric and Mom on our couch, except that she was crying.

It was Pastor Eric's turn to blurt, "It's not what you think!"

Then, Mom reached her arms out to me and whispered through her tears, "It's much, much better."

That's when she told me the amazing news about her salvation. Pastor Eric had congratulated Mom and given her the gift. Then, I heard him quietly shut the door behind him as he gave us time alone to celebrate together.

The doorbell rang, pulling me out of my reverie. I knew Mom would let whoever it was in, but I quickly finished putting things back and looked at my clock. It was a little early for the teens. Just as I got up, there was a knock on my door and Missy peeked in.

"I'm sorry I'm early," she said timidly, "but I wanted to share something with you before the others got here."

She definitely had my attention then. I shut my door behind her and sat down in my desk chair to wait for the news. From the excitement radiating from her as she sat on the edge of my bed, I knew it must be something intense.

"I just have to tell you about this crazy dream I had last night! In the dream, I was sitting at my desk working on my homework, then the walls of my bedroom... they just, they crumbled around me..."

Epilogue

THE BELL CLANGS loudly as I walk into the beauty parlor and a take a seat in one of the black, plastic chairs, arranged in a U. Two others are already waiting; not for my Beatrice, I hope. I don't have all day to sit around this place; besides, I can't tolerate the smell of those perm chemicals. Thankfully, I was blessed with naturally curly hair and don't have to be a fake.

One of my fellow patrons is a nicely dressed elderly woman, about the age of my mother. She's sitting to my left under the large picture window, wringing her hands on her purse strap, nervously. I guess she doesn't like waiting either. I've seen her around town often enough but don't know her personally—not unexpected since she doesn't go to my church. She startles me by asking for the *Good Housekeeping* magazine on the little table beside me. When I hand it over, she thanks me and admires my bracelet. It was a birthday present from my son, I tell her. What I don't say is that they're real diamonds. That would be tacky. I do mention my son's a doctor. She looks rightly impressed and turns her attention to the magazine.

Across from me, a teenage girl stares out the window, ears plugged up. I don't know how they can hear a thing, having that loud music pumped into their brains all of the time. I look over at her tight jeans and send a silent snarl of disapproval her way. A little shock runs through me when she takes out her plugs and looks my way. I didn't think she could see me. After giving her a sideways glance, I realize she's not looking at me at all. She's staring off in space, right past me. I fidget in the uncomfortable chair and watch her as she sends a questioning look to the old woman, who is paying her no mind at all. The girl looks past me again, this time closing her eyes for a minute as her mouth moves silently, like in prayer. Yep, she's a weird one. She lets out a deep breath then moves over to the seat right by the woman. Then she whispers in her ear, so quietly I can't make out a word. The old woman heard though because she looks surprised and a little scared at what was said. I lean a little closer in their direction to grab a magazine.

"How did you know?" the woman whispers in a shocked voice, loud enough for me to hear this time.

"I know the One who knows when a sparrow falls. He just wants you to know He cares," the teenager says and pats the woman's arm tenderly.

I see the big ring on her pointer finger. From the size of it, it would have to be a boy's class ring. His letterman jacket is by her on the empty chair. I strain to make out the details. I have to get these eyes checked soon. It has the number of that nice quarterback on it. This must be that girl who had such a wild streak in her; the one Malone had been warning people about a couple of months ago. Of course, now that rumor has it he may be prosecuted for the unspeakable, who could put a grain of trust in that man? I look back at the two and wonder why, if the girl was so evil, would she be holding that old lady's hand and talking to her so sweetly? Unless, she just wants something from her. I edge over in my seat a little to tune back in to their conversation. The other women in my group will want a full report. I haven't let them down yet.

"The...the problem began after Arthur, my husband, passed two years ago," I hear the old woman say. I have to really strain to make out what she chokes out next.

"I...I've tried to stop...I just can't seem to...stop myself."

"You must miss him," the teenager says, ignoring the strange confession and opening herself up for an earful instead.

Sure enough, the old woman launches into her long, sob story. I must have dozed off, because I give a little jump when I hear the manicurist call, "Amber" or maybe, "Ember." Those two stand up and the old woman tears up as she tells the girl goodbye.

"I'm getting my nails done for Homecoming. Why don't you come back with me and have yours done too? My treat," the teen offers.

The old lady giggles like a silly schoolgirl then glances my way. My face must show my true feelings about her behavior, because she has the good sense to flash a look of guilt my way. That doesn't stop her from heading on to the back with the girl, though. The infuriating bell jingles again, but I close my eyes to give them a rest. Those fumes give me a headache.

Next thing I know, Beatrice is giving a hard shake to my shoulder. I almost come out of my chair. She is telling me it's time for my color appointment. I don't know why she has to announce it to the world. I'm about to give her a piece of my mind when she dangles my bracelet in front of my face.

"Is it yours, Mrs. Nelson?" she asks me. "It was lying here on the seat beside you."

I grab it from her to hide my irritation and confusion. I don't know how it could've gotten off my wrist. *Real* diamond bracelets have very secure clasps. I stand up to follow her back. That's when I see those two, the old lady and teenager, outside. They hold up their nails and examine them as they walk past, smiling as if they're the best of friends. Like I said, weird.

Acknowledgments

I would like to thank: my husband for his unfailing confidence in me and for financing my reading habit, without him there would be no book; the Creation House team who saw something special in the story and put it all together; my sister who helped make it better; and Christ, my Savior; without Him there would be no me.

About the Author

....

Tammy is a homemaker with a love for reading, photography, and writing. A few years ago, she and her husband decided to trade an ordinary, comfortable life for a full life in Christ. This book is just one of the many exciting results of that decision. She and her husband have six children, three of whom have "left the nest." They live in the South of France with their three youngest daughters and two poodles.

Contact the Author

....

Tammy would love to hear from you!
You can e-mail her at:
e-mail@aseriesofgifts.com,
or visit her website:
www.aseriesofgifts.com
for all of the latest news and more ways to connect.